EMERALD
AISLE

EMERALD AISLE

A Notre Dame Mystery

RALPH MCINERNY

 St. Martin's Minotaur ∞ New York

www.minotaurbooks.com

Library of Congress Cataloging-in-Publication Data

McInerny, Ralph M.
    Emerald Aisle / Ralph McInerny.
        p. cm.
    ISBN 0-312-26938-2
    1. Knight, Roger (Fictitious character)—Fiction. 2. Knight, Philip (Fictitious character)—Fiction. 3. Private investigators—Indiana—South Bend—Fiction. 4. University of Notre Dame—4. Fiction. 5. South Bend (Ind.)—Fiction. 6. College teachers—Fiction. 7. Weddings—Fiction. I. Title.

PS3563.A31166 E4 2001
813'.54—dc21

                                          2001041945

First Edition: November 2001

10 9 8 7 6 5 4 3 2 1

For Pam & Gerry Bradley

EMERALD AISLE

PROLOGUE

SEVERAL YEARS AGO, TOWARD the end of the last millennium, two young undergraduates fell in love and decided to marry—marry eventually, but not immediately. Larry Morton and Dolores Torre were second semester freshmen at the time, with years of education before them. They had come to Notre Dame with the intention, firm in his case, vague in hers, of going on to law school after graduation, ideally at Notre Dame, thus becoming, in the phrase, double domers.

They met in a philosophy class in the Program of Liberal Studies but had been mere acquaintances for weeks until a clash over the meaning of the death of Socrates brought them together. Dolores insisted that Socrates had committed suicide; Larry maintained that he had been unjustly executed by the state.

"He drank the hemlock himself."

"He had no choice."

"No one forced him to drink it."

"That was the sentence."

"But he executed it himself. I say that someone who executes his own death sentence is a suicide."

The argument continued after class, across the campus, to Reckers and after that to Howard Hall where Dolores lived. Larry roomed in Dillon, just across the mall. They sat in the lounge of Howard and each decided to postpone the debate until the other overcame the dementia he or she momentarily was in the grips of.

He was from Minneapolis; she was from Phoenix. How did she

like Notre Dame? How did he? He wouldn't have gone anywhere else.

"I was so afraid I wouldn't be admitted."

Larry who had some experience of her mind expressed surprise.

She pretended to ignore this. "I thought they had a quota on girls, Larry."

"They do. One girl to every boy."

"No one told me who mine is."

"That's why I'm here. This is an official visit."

In jokes begins responsibility. They became inseparable. They fell in love. They decided to marry. To seal the bargain, since a formal engagement seemed premature, they spoke to the rector of the Basilica of the Sacred Heart on campus.

"We want to reserve a day for our wedding."

Father Rocca widened his eyes. "What year are you in?"

"Freshman."

His manner became avuncular. "Have you talked to Campus Ministry about marriage preparation classes?"

"We are thinking of June 2002."

The priest laughed. "But that's years from now."

"We want to make sure we'll be married here."

"Our schedule is crowded but . . ." He paused and his manner became as serious as theirs. "Well, okay. But I don't have a calendar for that far ahead."

"Saturday, June 17. We looked it up."

"Where did you find a 2002 calendar?"

"On the web."

He let it go. "I suppose if people register their babies with the Admissions Office as soon as they're born, this isn't really too odd."

The weddings of alumni in the campus church, and in the Log

Chapel were a regular feature of the spring and summer at Notre Dame. Larry's parents had been married in Sacred Heart.

"But your mother couldn't have gone here," the priest said.

"Saint Mary's. It was the same thing then."

"That was my fallback choice," Dolores said.

Father Rocca provided them with an official recognition of their reservation for June 17, 2002, a note written on Basilica stationery, since he did not have a date book for that distant year.

"God knows if I'll still be rector here when the time comes, but this will seal it."

They made a photocopy of the letter and argued over who should have the original.

"Take it, Dolores. You're less likely to lose it."

"Lose it!"

"You know what I mean."

"I can't tell the copy from the original anyway."

They continued to be inseparable into their sophomore year but then began to draw apart. Near Easter, by mutual consent and somewhat sadly, they broke up. They continued to see one another on occasion. Two years later, at graduation, they hugged and said good-bye and for a moment it seemed that things might start up again. But the moment passed.

"I'm going to work for West Publishing in Saint Paul," Dolores said.

"I enter law school in the fall."

"Here?"

"Where else?"

PART ONE

THERE WAS A BUMPER STICKER
Roger Knight saw around the campus on
game days when fans flowed in from across the land. GOD MADE
NOTRE DAME #1. The claim was theologically impeccable so long as
one had in mind the Lady after whom the university was named and
not the university itself, still less one of the varsity teams. A statue
of the eponymous Notre Dame graced the golden dome, a huge
effigy visible for miles around, the emblem of the university named
for her: Notre Dame du Lac, to be exact, Our Lady of the Lake. Or
rather to be inexact, since there were two campus lakes, Saint
Joseph's and Saint Mary's. But if the great golden dome and the
statue of the Virgin atop it were visible from the ground, they were
even more so from the air. Flights coming into South Bend followed
a landing pattern that brought them in low over the campus, and
pilots liked to give their passengers an extended view.

"There she is, folks, Notre Dame."

Thus spoke the pilot of the commuter plane Roger and his
brother, Phil, were flying in on from Chicago, propeller driven,
cramped, a notch or two above a hang glider. Roger was wedged
into two seats, the armrest between them raised, with Phil across
the aisle. The little plane had headed immediately out over Lake
Michigan when it took off from O'Hare and had stayed over the
great lake until a few minutes before entering the pattern that took
it over the campus.

"That's the stadium!" cried the pilot, and those with window seats dutifully pressed their noses against the glass and looked. "And that's the golden dome. See that statue on top of it? That's Knute Rockne, the famous football coach."

Roger looked at Phil. "He can't be serious, Roger."

But apparently he was serious. Perhaps he thought the statue was of Rockne in academic garb.

The pilot would not be the first one to mistake the athletic excellence of the university for its central purpose. This year God had indeed made Notre Dame #1 in both senses. Its academic ranking had risen into the top ten, a fact featured on the home page of the university web site, to the chagrin of senior faculty computer literate enough to have noticed it.

"What in hell is *U.S. News & World Report?*"

"A lesser *TIME.*"

"What is time?"

"The measure of motion," broke in a philosopher, and cackled.

Apart from the questionable legitimacy of such academic ranking, the varsity teams had excelled in every sport. The football team, after half a dozen years of drought, had ended its season playing for the national championship. Alas, they lost, but loyal fans attributed this to the outrageous officiating. Whatever wounds the loss inflicted were soon healed by the performance of the basketball teams, women's and men's, both of which were said to be headed for the Final Four. Even hockey, that poor brother of the Joyce Athletic Center, had swept its divisional play-offs, but this success melted away before the ascendancy of the basketball teams.

The two aspects of the university were loved unequally by the Knight brothers. When Roger had been offered the Huneker Chair of Catholic Studies, he had been flattered and delighted. He had not taught after receiving his doctorate from Princeton as a precocious nineteen year old. His enormous weight and eccentric manner had stood in the way of an academic career, and after a stint in the navy, where he ballooned to a size that earned him an early discharge, he lived with Phil and eventually became, like him, a private detective. They had been working out of Rye, New York, whither they had moved after Phil had been mugged in Manhattan for the third time. That one whose investigative services were his bread and butter should himself be unsafe on the streets of the metropolis did not seem a good marketing line. From Rye, Phil began to run an ad in the phone directories of various major cities, giving only an 800 number and accepting only those clients who offered a particular challenge and one that did not pose too great a difficulty for Roger's participation. Their's had been a pleasant life, active and lucrative enough for their purposes, and allowing Roger to pursue his myriad intellectual interests and carry on an enormous E-mail correspondence with kindred souls around the globe. The offer from Notre Dame, a welcome and unlooked for surprise, had meant the end of their life in Rye.

"Of course you'll take it," Philip had cried.

"But the agency?"

"I can work from anywhere, Roger. Clients don't know we live in Rye unless we tell them. South Bend might be even more convenient."

Roger was not deceived. Phil lifted the notion of sports fan to hitherto unknown heights, and he had long followed the fortunes of Notre Dame with a close and biased eye. Moving to South Bend ranked for Phil just below the beatific vision. His enthusiasm removed Roger's hesitation. Roger himself had looked forward to the library and the stimulation of his new colleagues, to say nothing of the prospect of teaching.

And so they had come to Notre Dame. The few years of their residence had rooted them in the university to such a degree that it took an effort of memory to think of a time before this.

9

Their flight from Chicago touched down, and the passengers straggled into the terminal. Roger took up his vigil by the baggage carousel, while Phil went to fetch the van from long-term parking. The vehicle had been remodeled so as to accommodate Roger's bulk. A rotating chair in the middle of the van, behind Phil in the driver's seat, enabled Roger to maneuver like a swivel gunner in World War II. A laptop was anchored to a table and thus out of use when he turned to the back, but he could easily swing east and west and then forward to chat with Phil. But on the ride from the airport this day, both brothers were quiet.

"I want a nap," Phil murmured.

"You deserve it."

Joseph Primero, a prospective client in Minneapolis, whose collection of rare books was destined for Notre Dame, had wanted to interview Philip, and vice versa, and Roger had gone along in order to see Primero's collection. For the nonce, he too could use some rest. But when they pulled up in front of their apartment, located in one of the buildings making up the graduate student village, a horn sounded and Nancy Beatty hopped out of her car and hurried toward them.

"Where have you two been! I was so worried about you."

Phil looked at Roger. "We've been away."

"That explains why your phone wasn't answered. It just rang and rang with no beep to leave a message. Larry wouldn't let me call Campus Security."

It was a pleasant thought that their absence had caused such concern. It was still a novelty for the Knight brothers to have people who worried about them.

"Where's Larry?"

Her eyes rolled upward. "Studying."

"Would you like to come in?"

She thought about it, then shook her head. "No. You're tired. But after this, let someone know when you're going away. Where have you been?"

"Minneapolis."

"Can I help with those?"

Phil had begun to unload their bags from the van. The thought of this frail girl helping him with the luggage brought a frown.

"It was just a thought." She paused. "I do have something to tell you."

"Come on in."

Again she shook her head. "Not now. I want Larry with me when I tell you."

"Can I guess?"

"Don't you dare."

2   ➤   NANCY   BEATTY'S   FATHER
taught in the History Department and that
meant she paid only room and board, her tuition covered as a faculty perk. But after freshman year, there was a proviso that she had to work a number of hours each week in return, so she had found a job in the law library, which is how she had met Larry Morton in her senior year. He was then in his third year of law school. The summer before he had interned in a Minneapolis firm and had been offered a job there after graduation.

"How would you like to live in Minneapolis?" he asked Nancy.

"Why do you ask?"

"Why do you think?"

And so they had become engaged.

"A lawyer?" her father had queried.

"He's a wonderful young man," her mother said.

Her parents met his when they visited campus, and they got along. Mr. Morton was in salt, the kind that is strewn on icy roads in Minnesota during the winter months. There were five Morton children of whom Larry was the oldest; and Mrs. Morton, a still beautiful woman whom childbearing had made more beautiful, decided that Larry had made an excellent choice. But Nancy's father was more grudging in his approval. "I thought you were going to graduate school."

She had been admitted to every program for which she had applied, something that filled her professorial father with pride. He obviously found it difficult to believe that she would turn aside from a promising academic career.

"I can take some courses in Minneapolis."

This did not mollify Professor Beatty. He knew all about part-time students. But Nancy's interest in graduate work had waned. She had heard her father's grumbling over the years and knew that all was not idyllic in the groves of academe. Being Larry's wife was future enough for her. Besides, she could go on with the life of the mind in the way Prof. Roger Knight had done before coming to Notre Dame.

"Roger Knight!" Her father was wary of the hotshots brought in from time to time by the administration, a practice that was not exactly a vote of confidence in the faculty members who had borne the heat of the day in the lean years as well as in the more recent fat ones.

"I wish you would make an effort to get to know him."

"He knows where my office is."

Professor Beatty's office was a warren in Decio, cluttered with books and papers and the mechanical typewriter he had bought years before as a graduate student. When she told him of Roger Knight's devotion to the computer, his brow clouded. "I'm not surprised."

Nancy had read of the Luddites who had tried to stop the Industrial Revolution by destroying machinery. Her father would willingly have taken an axe to all the computers on campus where students spent more time than they did among the books in the library.

"Dad, they're all available on the computer."

He just looked at her. Books and computers did not belong in the same sentence.

Nancy told Roger Knight of her father, and one day the huge

Huneker Chair of Catholic Studies knocked on Professor Beatty's door in Decio. A cloud of tobacco smoke emerged when the door opened, and a young female instructor who was passing in the hall coughed dramatically and brought a Kleenex to her face.

"Professor Beatty? Roger Knight."

The meeting became a legend in the family. The two men hit it off immediately. Her father had not known of Roger Knight's book on Baron Corvo and their conversation had centered on the last decade of the nineteenth century, the period of the *Yellow Book,* when platoons of aesthetes had joined the Catholic Church, not least among them Oscar Wilde. But it was a shared interest in Ronald Firbank that clinched the new friendship. Professor Beatty had despaired of ever having a colleague who knew the work of Firbank.

"He influenced Waugh."

"Powell wrote about him."

"His style is exquisite. His work, like his person, was more style than substance."

"Wodehouse."

And so it had gone on. Nancy was delighted. Of all her professors, Roger Knight was the one who had influenced her most. She had taken every course he offered, getting special permission if they were graduate courses. She was writing her senior essay on F. Marion Crawford, and of course she had brought Larry to meet the overweight genius.

"What kind of law will you practice?"

"Trusts."

"Ah."

Actually, Larry got along better with Philip Knight, with whom he could exchange arcane lore about Notre Dame athletics. When Larry gave Nancy a diamond, Roger Knight was the first one after her parents to be told. They had come to the Knight brothers' apartment the day after the brothers returned from Minneapolis to make the announcement. Neither of the brothers was married, but they approved of the institution and were appropriately congratulatory.

"If it is seemly to congratulate a future bride."

"Just don't commiserate with her," Larry said.

"When is the big date?"

"June 17. I hope you'll be here."

"You'll marry on campus?"

"Of course."

$\left(3\right)$ ⟶ IN HIS SEVENTH YEAR ON campus, Larry Morton was at last emotionally prepared for his departure. He would leave Notre Dame with a new wife and a great job awaiting him in Minneapolis. All the years of study now seemed worthwhile. His father was finally reconciled to the fact that Larry would not take over his business, but at least he was returning to his native state.

"If salt lose its savor," Professor Knight murmured.

Larry said nothing. He had become used to such "gnomic utterances" (Nancy's phrase) from the professor. Often Larry went off with Phil to basketball and hockey games while Nancy visited with Roger. Afterward they would gather in the Knight apartment where Roger would make popcorn while Larry and Phil rehearsed the game and Nancy and her favorite professor would continue with their own conversation. It was clear that Nancy would miss these sessions with Roger Knight, but Minneapolis was not a million miles away and she would be coming back from time to time to see her parents. It was understood that she would model her life, to the degree possible, on the preacademic years of Roger Knight.

"You mustn't confuse learning with education or with being on a campus."

Nancy nodded. Had she ever disagreed with Roger Knight? There had been a time, blessedly brief, when Larry had felt jealous of the huge man's influence on Nancy. But after all, it was Knight's example that had decided her against graduate school, something that would probably have postponed their marriage since she had planned on attending Northwestern.

Nancy had been surprised when Larry told her that they could be married in Sacred Heart.

"Don't they have a waiting list?"

"I was lucky."

"You should have taken me with you."

But he did not want to explain to her that he had secured the date years ago and why. He had not seen Dolores Torre since graduation, and Nancy knew nothing of her. There seemed no need to explain the youthful love that he and Dolores had thought would lead to marriage. How different it had been from what he felt for Nancy. Sometimes he missed the uncalculated way in which he and Dolores had plunged into talk of marriage. He had had a cool head when he'd proposed to Nancy, but then he was older now by half a dozen years. He had not as yet spoken with Father Rocca, but he had the copy of the note the priest had given him, assuring him that he could marry in Sacred Heart on June 17, 2002. One day he decided to drop by the Basilica and confirm the reservation.

"The young woman lives elsewhere?" Father Rocca asked, as if explaining to himself why the prospective groom had come alone to his office.

"I just wanted to make sure June 17 is all set."

"This June!"

"Yes."

The priest opened a ledger and began to flip pages. He found what he was looking for and then looked abjectly at Larry.

"June 17 is all booked."

"One of the weddings will be mine."

"But there is no way . . ."

That is when Larry showed the priest the note Father Rocca had written years before. Father Rocca read it and then looked uncomfortably at Larry. "What is your fiancée's name?"

"Beatty. Nancy Beatty. Her father is in the English Department."

"But this note says Dolores Torre."

"We broke up."

"Larry, Dolores is getting married here on June 17. I remember it now. She showed me this same note when she confirmed the date."

Larry left the rector's office in a daze and wandered toward the lake. How could he explain this to Nancy? Canada geese and ducks provided a sound track for his jumbled thoughts.

Relief came two days later while he was still trying to think of a way to break the news to Nancy that they would not be married in Sacred Heart. The truth was he couldn't accept the loss of that reservation. He had as much right to it as Dolores. And then came the call from the firm in Minneapolis he would join in June. Could he come up for a seminar offered to new lawyers in the firm. Immediately, he left a message for Dolores.

4   W H E N S H E F O U N D L A R R Y
Morton's message on her answering machine
at work, Dolores had felt a little lurch inside at having the past
invade the present.

*"I'll be in Minneapolis on Thursday and would like to see you. If
this is impossible, let me know. I'll come by for you at noon."*

Just like that. But of course Dolores had a sudden suspicion why
Larry would get in touch with her after all these years. She had felt
sneaky when she claimed the reserved date at Sacred Heart Basilica that she and Larry had made so long ago. It had almost surprised her that she still remembered it; but when Dudley, her
fiancé, had mentioned a Notre Dame wedding he had attended
while they were discussing their own plans, Dolores remembered
the visit to Father Rocca when she and Larry had told the rector
that they wanted to reserve June 17, 2002, for their wedding. There
were times when she thought that setting the date had been the
beginning of the end between her and Larry. It was one thing to fall
in love with a classmate and have someone to go out with, but the
prospect of marriage had been sobering and, with time, suffocating.
Graduation no longer loomed as a door into a vast unknown future
but only the prospect of returning to campus for three years of law,
after which she and Larry would be married in Sacred Heart. It was
as if her life was already over.

Of course this realization came on gradually, and she continued
to like Larry. He had been smart and fun and impressive in the

ordered way he lived his life. She didn't stop liking him, loving him even; but she simply wasn't ready to get married, to Larry or anyone else, until giving up her job with West and joining a Minneapolis law firm as assistant to Dudley Fyte had changed all that. Kunert and Skye had contracted with her to computerize their files and records on the model of West's huge legal databases. Within a week, she seemed to fit into the firm as if she had been there for years. She was receptive when Dudley broached the subject of her staying on permanently.

Dudley was ten years older than she, already a partner at Kunert and Skye, and obviously the hotshot of the firm.

"It happens as often as not," he had said to her, when several girls had informed him they were leaving to get married. "I factor it into my estimates of strength in this division. A woman will work, often extraordinarily well, for a few years, and then she leaves."

Dudley seemed to see this as a problem amenable to a computer-ized solution. Dolores felt that she should say something on behalf of her sisters in the firm, but the fact was that she almost envied the women who were leaving to marry.

"You could work for a while after you marry," Dolores suggested to one of them, Josie.

"I began a savings plan just so I wouldn't have to do that. I want a house, I want a garden, I want kids."

Josie's eyes lit up as she talked. Obviously, working had been merely a stage on life's way for her, and now that stage was over. Dolores thought of a house in the suburbs, a garden, kids. Suddenly it all seemed overwhelmingly attractive.

"You can always hire replacements," Dolores said to Dudley.

"Correction. *You* can. I want you to make the original cuts among the applicants, whittle the number down to ten or so, and bring them in for an interview. When you have reduced the possibles to three, I'll decide."

This was responsibility indeed, and one she didn't particularly relish. Being assistant to Dudley apparently made her a jill-of-all-trades. Looking over the applications, particularly those from young women just finishing college, it occurred to Dolores that her own application, despite her previous work experience, had been reviewed like this only a few years ago. Of course there was nothing on the application to indicate how long the person intended to work. What had she herself thought when she sent in her application? The future had not seemed finite, but wide open, and going to work was the entry into that future. It seemed to her now that she had removed all plans of eventual marriage from her mind. If she had thought of it, it would have seemed an aspect of a future that began with taking a job. Most working women are married, aren't they? And vice versa. Dudley's matter-of-fact remark about the longevity of women in the workforce made her realize that she would no longer want to go on working after she married. Like Josie, it seemed, she had come to think of work as preparation for marriage.

She asked Dudley if he would like her to try unobtrusively to get a sense of how long women applicants intended to work.

"Better not. Besides, they wouldn't know."

"You've become quite an expert on the subject."

"Let's discuss it over dinner."

Dinner with the boss. Well, well. Of course it would be just business. Maybe he was just being ultracareful, not discussing such a delicate subject as women employees in the office. Nonetheless, for the rest of the day she took notice of Dudley in a way she really hadn't before. "Distinguished" was the word that came to mind, followed by intelligent, ambitious, a little vain. He seemed to be studying her as well. Several times their eyes almost met. For heaven's sake. Dolores made herself scarce until they would leave the office for the restaurant.

"How long do you intend to work?" he asked, far along in the meal, with the glow of two cocktails upon them and a portly Italian waiter whose hovering somehow did not seem to matter. His English was apparently confined to the items on the menu.

"I haven't given it much thought."

"No fiancé? No special friend?"

The career girl she thought she was would have stopped him right there. He had no right to pry into her private life and ask such personal questions, but the sense that he was her boss seemed to have deserted both of them.

"I was engaged in college. Nothing came of it."

"You broke up."

"Uh huh. It really wasn't serious."

"I should think an engagement was very serious."

"Not when you're that young. It was like going steady."

"I never went steady."

"That's hard to believe."

Even harder to believe was the way that one dinner altered forever their attitude toward one another. He asked her out a lot after that, to plays, to music, to exhibits, to baseball games when the Sox played the Twins. They attended Josie's wedding together, and Dolores envied the bride's radiant beauty.

"Now she'll have her house and garden and kids."

"Do you ever think about such things?"

"Of course."

"Of quitting work and marrying and all the rest?"

"I'd have to have an offer."

"Of course."

He made his offer later that day. They had both drunk deep of Josie's champagne, but their heads seemed clear as bells. Dolores caught the bridal bouquet when Josie tossed it into a throng of unmarried women, having to lunge to get it; and she was holding it like a bride when Dudley kissed her for the first time.

"Hey, I'm the bride," Josie said. "You're supposed to kiss me." She puckered up and leaned toward Dudley, who obliged.

"That's the first time I've kissed a married woman. I look forward to making a habit of it." And he kissed Dolores again.

That was the first version of his proposal. It was just fine with Dolores. In subsequent days they started to make their plans. When the site of the wedding came up, Dudley mentioned a wedding held at Notre Dame that had impressed him.

"That's where we're going to get married."

"Is that a perk of alumni?"

"Nae."

"It's not?"

"Alum*nae* as well as alumni."

"I was using it inclusively."

"That's Alums."

She called Father Rocca and reminded him of the time she had reserved for her wedding on June 17. He made a note in the registry, and it was all set. She and Dudley would get married on June 17 at ten in the morning in Sacred Heart Basilica.

"And the groom is Lawrence Morton?"

"No, Father. He changed his name to Dudley Fyte."

The rector was puzzled but didn't pursue it, and the date was secured.

And now she had received a message from Larry Morton, with whom years ago she had made that June 17 appointment, and he pretty well insisted on seeing her on Thursday.

(5) — — → AT THE WEDDING RECEP-
tion, when he said that Josie was the first
married woman he had kissed, Dudley was consciously lying. Jok-
ing too of course, but it was as if he wanted to erase the past completely and be what Dolores obviously thought he was.

When he first realized how fascinated he was by Dolores, he had
not expected it to go anywhere. His relationship with Bianca
Primero, stormy but satisfying, was all he could handle. And it left
him free. He and Bianca could never have more than they now had.

Dolores had been hired to put computerized order into the records,
files, and billing of the firm, hired by Kunert himself; but immediately Dudley had noticed her independence and humor compared to
the anxious young lawyers in the annual crop of new hires, the seri-
ous-faced young men not yet at ease in business suits, the young
women trying to assume the blasé look of the professional woman. Of
course, in the byzantine hierarchy of Kunert and Skye, Dolores out-
ranked the other newcomers as assistant to Dudley Fyte. She had first
caught Dudley's attention because she had something in short supply
in the office, an outrageous sense of humor. He himself had none.

"How was your weekend?" he asked her.

"I wear a hat over the weak end."

He stared at her.

"It's an old vaudeville joke, according to my father."

"How old is your father?"

She squinted at him. "Older than you."

"Hey, I could be your older brother."

"You'll have to talk to my mother about that."

Not an auspicious beginning of anything, but there was something about her subdued sassiness that reminded him of Bianca. It was Bianca who had made him immune to the attractions of the women in the office, who by contrast seemed impossibly young and naive. He himself had felt that way with Bianca at first.

He had met Bianca Primero last year in Highland Village in a gallery to which he had been drawn by a painting in the window, blues and whites and soft yellows, a woman on a beach, holding her daughter with one hand and her shoes in the other. He went in, he paused before every picture, all of which conveyed the mood of the painting that had drawn him inside. What was the mood?

"Sentimentality."

The woman who said this wore a black lace mantilla over her golden hair, and her arms were crossed over a loose, yellow raincoat. She looked at Dudley when he turned to her, but her large, opaque sunglasses gave him back diminished images of himself.

"I like the colors," he said.

"Primary colors. When did you last see a red sail?"

"In the sunset."

She removed her glasses with a slow, dramatic movement. Her lips slowly formed a smile.

"So you like sentimental songs as well?"

"Dudley Fyte," he said, and thrust out his hand. She hesitated, then took it.

"Bianca Primero."

"You don't like this show."

"I didn't say that. I said the pictures are sentimental. I have nothing against sentimentality."

There was an odd, guarded intimacy in her tone. He decided that this was what one expected of a Saturday morning, meeting a beautiful older woman in an art gallery and falling into conversation. They looked at other pictures, she murmuring disapproval with little sighs, he defending the pictures.

"Would you care for coffee?"

"In a minute," she said, and signaled to the director, who hurried obsequiously over to her.

"Yes, Mrs. Primero?"

"That one." She pointed toward the picture that had elicited her judgment of sentimentality. She opened a purse and gave the director a card.

"You'll deliver it."

"Of course."

"Telephone first." Now she handed him a credit card. It occurred to Dudley that she had not asked the price of the painting.

They sat at a sidewalk table up the street and sipped espresso. Bianca wore her large sunglasses and surveyed the passersby with a world-weary air.

"I'm just back from Capri."

"Ah."

"Do you know it?"

"Only by reputation."

The glasses were removed. "That sounds prudish."

Dudley had read a life of Krupp, the armament tycoon who had spent time on the legendary isle. "It has always attracted tyrants, illicit lovers, and perverts," she said.

"And which are you?"

"Not the last."

Before they parted she gave him one of her cards. Three days later he telephoned her. "You said to call first."

His name seemed to mean nothing to her; but when he mentioned the gallery, she said languidly, "The picture has been delivered. You must come admire it."

When she opened the door, she stepped back; and when he came inside, she gave him her cheek to kiss. Her golden hair was pinned up, and she wore a flowing floor-length muumuu. As she crossed the room, the garment caught the outline of her body then billowed free in a way that Dudley found seductive. That of course was the idea. She led him to the picture and put her arm through his as they looked at it. She said nothing. He turned to her, and she lifted her face. The kiss was the beginning of far more than Dudley had bargained for.

Later, she wanted to know all about him, as if to justify the impetuosity with which she had led him down a hallway to her bedroom. She listened as she might have to one with an exotic story.

"I would never have taken you for a lawyer. Are you married?"

"Are you?"

"I'm on leave."

"I'm not married."

"I guessed that."

Was she criticizing his performance? He did not pursue it. He sought and found the appropriate tone to tell her of the young women who worked for him.

"Suited but not suitable?"

"They're so young."

She frowned and it was warning enough. The relationship developed the year before Dolores joined the firm, a year during which much had happened. Bianca might consider herself on leave from her marriage, but her husband did not.

Some months after his first meeting with Bianca, Joseph Primero came to see him at the office. When the girl told him the visitor's name, Dudley scrambled to his feet. He had no intention of meeting Bianca's husband in his office.

"I'll talk with him in a conference room."

This was a visit Bianca had prepared him for, warned him would come, but now that it had he was surprised and flustered.

"Hasn't he come to see you yet?" Bianca had asked when talk turned to her husband.

"You're kidding, aren't you?"

Bianca smiled. "Wait and see."

But any uneasiness Dudley felt had vanished as he went to meet Primero. A husband with a wandering wife was not in a strong position to make another man feel ashamed. Dudley was more embarrassed by the age difference between himself and Bianca than he was by the fact that she was married. Of course, he had checked up on Joseph Primero and been impressed, very impressed, by the man's accomplishments. Primero was wealthy and could afford to let Bianca travel, have an apartment in Highland Village, buy whatever she wanted, and be bored.

"You collect art; he collects books," Dudley said.

"That is not how he would put it. Collecting sounds like a hobby, a diversion; books are his passion."

"But he made his fortune as a real estate developer."

"It's a long story."

Dudley met Joseph Primero in the reception area, shook his hand with a distracted air, and led him down the hall to a conference room. When he closed the door behind them, he indicated a chair for Primero.

"You're younger than I had thought."

Dudley could think of nothing to say to that.

"I am not here to blame you. Bianca can be an irresistible force. I understand that."

Dudley felt like a gigolo, which doubtless was Primero's intention. But what else was he? The suggestion that he was a naive young man who had fallen into the clutches of a voracious older woman rankled. It was he who had initiated things with Bianca.

"Of course at first I didn't realize she was married," he said. "Not many married women manage to live so independently."

Primero looked away. The tinted windows gave a view of the skyline as a Lego arrangement. Primero rubbed his chin, then turned to Dudley. "Free yourself from her."

Dudley sat. "Do you have to make such visits often?"

Primero glared at him, and for a moment Dudley thought the older man might attack him. But then the expression of resigned sadness returned. "My visit was meant as a favor to you. Given the discrepancy in your ages, I don't suppose you would think of marriage. A good thing. She will never divorce me."

"She seems to have all she wants now."

"She will tire of you."

"We'll see." But he found that the prospect did not displease, as long as it was sometime in the future. A steady diet of Bianca Primero was wearing.

"I would have thought your sights would have been higher."

That seemed to be it. Back in his office, Dudley found himself feeling sorry for Bianca's cuckold husband.

"Who's Joseph Primero?" Amy asked.

"Not a client. A relative of a friend of mine."

How much did Amy know? Was he the subject of whispers in the ladies' room? If so, he didn't mind. He still regarded Bianca as a conquest, and her husband's visit increased her trophy value. But Joseph Primero did not look like a man who would willingly subject

30

himself to the humiliation of a wife run amok. And he underwrote the life Bianca led. She had no money of her own. Why didn't Primero divorce her?

Bianca laughed. "You don't understand us Catholics. But tell me what he said."

She wanted a blow-by-blow account of her husband's visit, rubbing her hands eagerly as he told her.

"Why do you hate him so?"

She sobered instantly and looked at Dudley with narrowed eyes. "You don't know him as I do. Besides, it is he who hates me."

"He has an odd way of showing it."

"I wish you had been harder on him. Imagine, coming to your office and asking you to leave me alone. The man has no pride."

"Maybe he loves you."

"He doesn't know what love is. Oh, I would like to punish him."

That became a leit-motif of their postcoital conversations. Sometimes Dudley thought that Bianca made love as a long-distance punishment of her husband.

"His books," she said, "that is where he is vulnerable."

She would lie back and speak dreamily of stealing from her husband's collection; she knew the things he particularly valued. Dudley became uneasy when she seemed to be casting him in the role of thief.

6 ➤ "LARRY," DOLORES SAID BRIGHTLY, "this is Dudley Fyte."

Larry had expected to talk to Dolores alone and was put off by the presence of the man to whom she had just introduced him, presumably the man she intended to marry in Sacred Heart Basilica. He took the extended hand, what else could he do?

"I've told Dudley about us."

"Why don't we all have a drink," Dudley suggested. And off they went across the lobby and out the door of the building. On the flight to Minneapolis, Larry had rehearsed what he would say to Dolores, convincing himself that he had the upper moral hand. After all, reserving a date for their wedding had been his idea. As he remembered it, Dolores had not been all that excited by the idea. Besides, how could she have the same emotional attachment to Notre Dame that he, after seven years on campus, had?

The bar was crowded. There was only one unoccupied stool and of course Dolores took that, with himself and Dudley standing attendance on her. Larry felt at a disadvantage. How could he even bring up the topic of June 17? But it was Dolores who did so.

"I wish now I'd let you know I was claiming the reservation."

"You should have." Of course he had not called her before going to the Basilica office to claim it himself.

"Well, it was as much mine as yours, wasn't it?"

"Was it? I thought it was my idea to make it in the first place."

"That isn't how I remember it."

Dudley reached for the drinks that had been brought, handing one to Dolores and taking his own. Larry's beer remained on the bar. He reached for it as Dudley proposed a toast. "I suppose we should offer one another mutual congratulations."

Larry lifted his glass but before drinking said, "Did you go to Notre Dame?"

"Chicago."

"Well then. My fiancée is a domer."

"How nice," Dolores said.

"That makes it two to one."

"Larry, everything is arranged."

"You're going to have to rearrange then." He drank now as if to punctuate the point.

"I don't think so. Father Rocca confirmed the date."

"He was under the mistaken impression that you and *I* were going to get married."

"I think the bride has the call in these matters."

"I don't see that."

"Larry, I understand how you feel. I know how I would have felt if I found you had gotten there before me. But the thing is done now, and it can't be undone."

He drank some more, trying in vain to remember the overpowering arguments he had formed on the flight up. "This isn't the place to discuss the matter."

"What is there to discuss? Say we each had an equal claim to the date; I got there first."

"Without telling me."

"But you found that out when you went to do the same thing."

"Ladies first, old man," Dudley Fyte said.

"Would you mind staying out of this?"

"I can hardly do that. I *am* involved. More than you are, I would say."

Dudley Fyte was a head taller, an older man, but one who looked fit as a fiddle. Nonetheless, it was hard to resist the impulse to take a swing at him. Dolores must have sensed Larry's anger. She put a hand on his arm and leaned toward him. "Larry, don't be upset. I really am sorry. How could I have known you had become engaged?"

She had been beautiful years ago, and she was more beautiful now. The pressure of her hand on his arm brought back memories of when they had been in love. Her expression of regret seemed genuine enough. If only Dudley hadn't been there.

"We should have talked about this alone."

"Larry, Dudley and I work together."

It seemed such an irrelevant remark, he laughed. "And you're settled in Minneapolis. You should have your wedding here."

"Now see here," Dudley began,

"Dudley, don't."

"Dolores, you have already gone an extra mile."

"I flew five hundred miles," Larry blurted out, feeling like a fool.

"On a pointless errand."

Dolores shifted her hand to Dudley's arm and shook her head. For a mad moment Larry thought that it was he and Dolores against this supercilious ass. "Could we discuss this alone, Dolores?"

She looked at him with affection, with something almost more than affection. She really did see his point. She looked at her attendant. "Dudley?"

"I think I should stay."

"Maybe it would be best if Larry and I talked alone."

He frowned. "You insisted I come and now I see why."

34

"What's that supposed to mean?" Larry asked.

"Dolores told me what she expected, and she was right."

Dolores looked back and forth at the two men, unsure what she should do. She had scarcely touched her drink.

"Where are you staying, Larry?"

"I'm at the Radisson."

Dudley said, "We'd better go, Dolores, I made a reservation"—he turned a small smile on Larry—"for dinner."

"Please don't be angry, Larry. It would spoil my wedding to think that you felt this way."

"Spoil the wedding?" Dudley laughed.

Again Larry felt an impulse to hit the other man, and this was like a concession of defeat. Dolores's hand was again on his arm. She had always been demonstrative. More memories came. He almost felt that Dudley was stealing his girl as well as the reservation at Sacred Heart. But then he remembered Nancy. Suddenly this trip seemed foolish. He put his glass on the bar. "It won't spoil my wedding." It was like a playground quarrel. "Good-bye."

But he stood there, wanting to say something more that would restore his sense of being in the right.

"Can't Father Rocca give you another day, Larry?"

"Sure, a couple of years from now."

That had to be his exit line. He turned to go.

"I'll pay for your beer," Dudley said.

Larry pulled out his wallet and threw a bill on the bar. A ten. But he would be damned if he would wait for change. He got to the door and pushed through and started rapidly up the street, wishing he hadn't made this stupid, doomed trip to Minneapolis. At the Radisson, he went upstairs to his room where he sat on the bed and reviewed the silly exchange in the bar.

What would he have said to Dolores if their roles had been

reversed? She had as much claim to the date as he did; but if he had nailed it down first, would he have withdrawn in her favor? Of course not. But it grated on him that it was Dudley Fyte as well as Dolores he was accommodating. And now where would he and Nancy marry?

After half an hour, he went downstairs to eat and then went to a bar off the lobby and ordered a drink he had a better chance of enjoying. He was still there when Dolores slipped onto the stool beside his.

"Hi."

He looked past her. "Are you alone?"

"It didn't seem like a good idea to bring Dudley."

"He's quite a guy."

"He really is, Larry."

"I don't know why I thought it made sense to come up here to talk with you about it."

"Did you really expect me to cancel?"

He would have liked to say what he thought of her marrying Dudley Fyte. If Fyte had been a more likeable man, it would have been easier to accept the loss of the June 17 reservation.

"Tell me about your girl, Larry."

So he did, a bit, but soon they were recalling their sophomore year together, the decision to marry, and sealing it by going over to Sacred Heart and making a claim for June 17, 2002. Had Dolores thought that was the date she would marry no matter what? Larry sometimes thought he had proposed to Nancy in order to be able to claim the reservation.

"Have you told her about us?"

"No."

"Why not?"

He shrugged.

"Didn't she wonder why you had a reservation at the Basilica?"

"I thought I would check first. That's how I found out that you . . ."

They moved to a booth and conversation came easily. Larry wondered what might have happened if they had met again before either of them had become engaged to someone else.

"We were so young, Larry."

"How old is Dudley?"

"Let's just talk about the past."

It was odd the things he remembered with Dolores seated across from him, leaning toward him, her eyes glistening as they recalled how it had been. From his position, Larry could see the entrance from the lobby, so when Dudley Fyte appeared and looked around the bar he saw him. Their eyes met and Larry tensed, figuring that Dudley would come in and make a scene, but he whirled on his heel and disappeared.

"What's the matter, Larry?"

He realized that his hands were covered by Dolores's. She had not seen her fiancé.

"Nothing."

7   CONFRONTED WITH A RIVAL
in Larry Morton, Dudley released from a
vault in his brain the memory of how an earlier rivalry had ended.
He and Ted Bonner had joined Kunert and Skye at the same time,
and it soon became clear that they were cast in the role of professional competitors. The contest had been exhilarating, spurring
himself and Bonner to better each previous performance as well as
one another's. But beneath it all was the sickening possibility of
failure—the logical possibility of failure. Dudley was certain he
would triumph, but doubts would come. So he made a friend rather
than an enemy of Bonner. They skied in Colorado, took a week at
Saint Kitts, sailed. That was how the rivalry came to an end.

Dudley still kept his boat, a twenty-four footer, in a marina at
Deephaven even after the tragedy. Of course it had been repainted
and refitted since that sad day when it had been discovered on its
side a thousand yards offshore in Lake Minnetonka, its sails in the
water causing it to turn in slow bewilderment as if in search of mag-
netic north. The boat had been empty. Dudley himself had sounded
the alarm when he managed to make it ashore, swimming through
the black, chill waters toward the lights of the boathouse. He had
come dripping into the bar like the old man of the sea.

"Good Lord," someone cried, "what happened to you?"

"My boat capsized."

It went without saying that the boat could not be righted without
assistance.

"Are you all right, Dudley?"

"Has my passenger come ashore?"

So it was that he made known the fact that Bonner had been with him in the boat. No one in the marina bar had seen Bonner. The bar emptied as everyone went down to the dock. The sound of motors began. Dudley, wrapped in a blanket, went out with a man named Armitage in his cruiser. The capsized boat had already been found when they got there, a shout going up and a spotlight playing over the floundering craft.

There was no sign of Bonner. Dudley's boat was righted and tied up behind Armitage's cruiser. But Dudley would not leave the scene. He blamed himself aloud for not remaining with the boat until he had found his passenger. "I told him to swim for shore when it went over."

"What could you have done in the dark?"

"I couldn't see much. I shouted and shouted. I wondered if he was already safe, but when I started for shore I felt I was abandoning him."

"Can't he swim?"

"He lost his grip and was pitched from the boat when it went over. I dove beneath it again and again . . ."

Someone wrapped the blanket more tightly around Dudley, who had begun to tremble. Armitage was urged to head for shore. The impact of what had happened, delayed during the activity of the futile rescue attempt, had now set in. Dudley sat in a crouch, swaddled in his blanket, staring sightlessly ahead, his teeth chattering like castanets.

Onshore he was taken to the emergency room but was released within an hour. Armitage stayed with him throughout it all.

"What did you say his name was?"

"Bonner. You've met him."

Armitage scratched his nose. "I don't remember."

"He works with me at Kunert and Skye. He was thinking of buying my boat. We took it out so he could get a sense of her."

"When was that?"

"After six."

Armitage raised his eyebrows.

"We were just going to take a turn or two and then come in for dinner."

Bonner had been delighted with the boat, and Dudley had turned the tiller over to him. Let the boat sell itself. He himself wanted either a larger boat or a cruiser like Armitage's. Sailing was all right, but it involved so much work before and after going out that he could not often find time for it. After maneuvering the boat, tacking, turning, letting the sails out and taking them in, even letting out the spinnaker as a strong breeze came up, they fixed the tiller and relaxed. Some talk about the boat—"I want it"—then inevitably about work.

"Has Kunert asked to talk with you?" Bonner asked.

"Talk with me?"

"I have an appointment with him tomorrow."

Dudley had no appointment with Kunert. A coldness came over him at the thought that he had lost to Bonner after all. Later, after the accident, he asked himself if he had subconsciously willed it to happen. Had he done everything he could have to save Bonner? He argued it both ways, prosecutor and counsel for the defense. It seemed a case that could never be decided. But one thing was clear. Bonner's untimely death had removed every obstacle to Dudley's rapid rise in the firm.

Bonner's body washed ashore miles east of the marina the following day. The wound on his head explained why he had not swum ashore like Dudley.

"He must have struck his head on something when the boat went over."

Dudley had been called to the scene and was led through the little crowd that ringed the body. An ambulance had been driven across the beach to where it lay. But Bonner was in need of a hearse rather than an ambulance. Dudley looked down at the colorless body, the matted hair, the wound on the side of the head. The last time he had seen Bonner, the young man had been alive and vigorous, moving agilely toward the front of the boat as he took in the spinnaker. He had wanted to prove to himself that he could handle the boat without a crew. But the spinnaker had been caught by a gust, the boat lurched, the tiller came loose, and before Dudley could control the boat it was tilting dangerously. And then, with a great, almost silent swoosh, it went over, and Bonner lost his balance, slid along the deck, and into the water. Dudley too was pitched into the water.

These memories came after Dudley met Dolores's former fiancé. A rival in the firm was one thing, but Larry Morton threatened Dudley's relationship with Dolores. His worry thus far had been that she would somehow find out about Bianca Primero, but now her old love had reappeared. There had been a slow maturation of Dudley's decision to pursue Dolores seriously. The half-serious deference she showed him in the office faded away when they were together. He catered to her love of music, they frequented museums, they attended plays. Dudley received a belated liberal education from the young woman who had attracted him from the beginning and seemed even more attractive now. But a full year passed before the day he proposed after Josie's wedding.

"We could have the wedding at Notre Dame," Dolores said.

"Anywhere you want."

"If we marry on June 17, that is."

He had not understood the meaning of the hypothetical until Dolores heard from Larry Morton and told him how she and Larry had reserved the date for their planned wedding and that she had claimed the date for her marriage to Dudley. Dudley didn't quite like the link between his marriage to Dolores and her old engagement to Morton, but it had seemed a small thing until the three of them were together in the bar.

He had expected Larry Morton to look like an undergraduate, but of course he was now finishing law school, where he had done well, and there was an air of confidence about him that would have commended him to Dudley if he were applying for a job in his firm; but in the bar he acted as if he had as much a claim on Dolores as on the reserved date in the campus church at Notre Dame.

Dudley had noticed when Dolores placed her hand on Morton's arm. She was a demonstrative woman, but the gesture seemed to evoke a romantic past that excluded him. He could not resist taunting Morton, trying to reduce him to the undergraduate status he had imagined him having. There was a moment when he was sure Morton would throw a punch at him, and Dudley almost wished he would. He was certain he would come out the better in any such encounter.

The meeting had not ended well. After Morton went off to the Radisson, Dolores was still upset by the encounter with her former fiancé.

"I feel so sorry for him, Dudley."

"He'll get over it."

"You don't know him like I do."

Again he felt excluded from something mysterious, something that had not stopped. Had meeting Morton again after all these years stirred up more than memories in Dolores?

"Let's go to dinner."

"Dudley?"—her hand was on his arm—"would you mind if we didn't? I'm afraid I wouldn't be good company for you."

"You're always good company."

She smiled, she gripped his arm, but she did not want to go to dinner. Outside he put her in a cab, and as it pulled away he had a dark thought. He hailed another cab. By then hers was lost in the traffic.

"Where to?"

"The Radisson."

He rode up and down the escalator, he sat in a chair in the lobby watching people come and go. Morton appeared and went into the bar off the lobby without noticing him. It was silly sitting there like a spy, but Dudley sat on. Since his worst fears were unrealized, he had half a mind to go into the bar and have a drink with Morton. There was no need to quarrel with him. But before he got up, Dolores suddenly appeared. She crossed the lobby to the desk. A phone call was made for her, and then the clerk shook his head. Another question and then he pointed toward the bar.

Dudley sat motionless in his chair as this silent drama went on. Dolores stood in the entrance of the bar for a moment and then disappeared inside. If she had come to mollify Morton, she must be motivated by something other than shared memories. The sight of him, talking with him, the way she had brushed aside his own objection to Morton—all these gathered together and gave Dudley the sinking feeling that he was in danger of losing the girl he loved.

He got up and in the entrance of the bar saw them: a couple, a couple in love, a couple engaged in talk that forever excluded him.

When his eyes met Morton's, he left, forcing himself to go, quashing the desire to stalk into the bar, lift Morton from his seat, and give him a thrashing.

Dudley went from the Radisson to Bianca's apartment. She was excited about a scheme to punish her husband. Removing books from her husband's collection (could also seem Dudley's personal response to Primero's calling on him at Kunert and Skye. For Bianca it went much deeper.

"Nothing could hurt him more."

That Primero should be hurt was an axiom with her. And didn't Primero invite such treatment? Dudley still could not believe that a man who had accomplished as much as Joseph Primero would permit his wife to treat him as she did.

"Maybe I'll explain it to you someday," Bianca said impatiently. "Right now, you have to steal the things on this list."

"Steal?"

Bianca dipped her head, then smiled. "Not *steal*. I will give you my key to the house; you will be my guest. The books would be considered common property, wouldn't they? You're the lawyer."

Dudley convinced himself that it was a practical joke they were playing on Primero. "What will you do with the stuff if I get it?"

"When, not if. I don't know what I'll do. It's his reaction I'm curious about."

She wanted to come with him to the house on Lake of the Isles, but he vetoed that. This had to be a quick in and out, even if it was just a practical joke. Primero himself was up north.

"Anyone else in the house, servants?"

She laughed. "A man with a beard, the curator of the collection;

he lives over the garage. He begins to drink immediately after dinner and is out like a light by ten."

"How would you know that?"

"He's a legend."

Approaching a house you intend to enter without an invitation, even if he had Bianca's keys, was a far different sensation than any Dudley had felt before. He had rehearsed a story if anything went wrong. He had come to pick up something for Mrs. Primero. Display of keys. In case of doubt, he would insist that she be called. He had gone through this with Bianca, who kept saying there was no need to worry; Waldo would be out like a light.

"Waldo?"

"The curator."

"Are there dogs?"

There were no dogs. It sounded almost too simple.

"When?" he asked.

"Why not tonight?" She pressed against him. "I'll wait for you."

Dudley parked several houses away and walked back to Primero's house. There were lights on, but Bianca had explained that: timers, security. But who would they fool? They could have fooled Dudley. He turned in the driveway, trying to make as little noise as possible. The windows in the apartment over the garage shone dimly, Waldo's apartment. Just before he got to the door, Dudley had a thought that stopped him. What if this were a practical joke Bianca was playing on *him*? He would sneak up to the door, let himself in, and the lights would go on, laughter burst out . . . No. That was crazy. He went around the house to the sunporch and pulled on the screen door. Was it stuck? He tried again. It was locked! He had no key to open screen doors; it was the door beyond that was supposed to be locked. His first reaction was that this absolved him from going on. He would beat it back to his car, explain it all to Bianca, and she would nag him until he came back another time.

He retraced his steps and came to what would be the door to a hallway leading to the kitchen. Bianca had drawn up a crude floor plan for him, but the designated point of entry was to have been the sunporch. That would have given him almost immediate access to the much-touted collection of books.

"What kind of books?"

"His favorite is Newman."

"Newman?"

"Cardinal Newman. Dudley, you don't have to understand."

There were two items on the list, each followed by its location in the library.

"You remember all that?"

"Some things you never forget."

There was no locked screen door to stop him now. He eased it open, got the right key into the lock, and turned it. The sound of the inner door as he pushed it open was magnified by the fact that he was holding his breath. He got inside, sought and deactivated the alarm, and then stood motionless. The longer he stood there, the more the house spoke to him—far off murmurs of clocks and air conditioners, a drop of water, creaking. How easy it was to imagine footsteps overhead. What if the curator was not drunk? What if he had noticed someone come up the driveway, go around to the sunporch, come back . . . ?

The choice was between going ahead or facing the mockery of Bianca if he returned without the items on her list. As he moved toward the library, he brought out the cloth bag Bianca had given him. "For the loot," she'd explained.

"You should be doing this, not me."

"It's man's work." And she pressed herself against him.

In the library he followed her instructions and found the items where she had said they would be. The book on the shelf and, in a wooden file cabinet near the window, second drawer from the top, the folder marked PAMPHLET EDITION. With the cloth bag full, he quickly left the house, trying not to run down the driveway. He got behind the wheel of his car and put his head back and breathed deeply for several minutes. Then he started the car and headed back to Bianca and his reward.

8 ROGER KNIGHT AND HIS

brother Phil flew off to Minneapolis in response to a call from Joseph Primero. On their previous visit, Primero had expressed concern about the security of his rare book collection but it had been unclear what service he expected Phil to provide. Now a theft had occurred and he wanted to hire a private investigator.

"Joseph Primero," Father Carmody had said at table the night before, perking up at the mention of the name.

"You know him?"

"Of course. He is a major benefactor of the university. He refused to have his own name put on the building his money made possible, so we called it Newman Hall. He has a great devotion to Cardinal Newman, as well as an interest in his writings, somewhat unusual for a man who has made his money building resorts on various northern Minnesota lakes.

"There are many Newman items in the Primero Collection," Roger said.

He knew the collection both from the brief visit he and Phil had made to Minneapolis some weeks before and from the duplicate catalog kept by Notre Dame. This was in anticipation of the eventual transfer of the books to the Hesburgh Library.

"Why on earth does he want to hire a detective?" Father Carmody asked.

The purpose of the first visit had been enigmatic, but the phone call that took them to Minneapolis a second time could not have been clearer. Primero had been robbed. Several extremely rare items were missing from his Newman Collection, a fact that had been brought to his attention by Waldo Hermes, the librarian and rare book man Primero had hired to preside over and extend his collection.

"I got the impression he suspects Hermes," Phil said.

"No!" Roger's impression of Hermes made it difficult to believe that the custodian would have stolen from the collection in his care. "Phil, you have to go up there."

"Only if you come along. The only Newman I know is the icon of *MAD* magazine.

It said something of the catholicity of Roger's interests that he did not require an explanation of what *MAD* magazine was. And since the midsemester break loomed, Roger agreed to accompany Phil to Minneapolis. This normally would have meant going in the van since Roger and airplanes made an imperfect match. Seats in planes had not been designed for one of his girth, and flying first class was disagreeably more expensive than coach. Unless of course the client paid their way, as Primero insisted on doing. So one day they had set off for the South Bend airport in the van.

Joseph Primero was short but imposing, a man whose manner and dress seemed a conscious negation of the fact that he was extremely wealthy. That he had done so well had come to him almost as a surprise. He had built his first resort in northern Minnesota near Mille Lacs with the intention of managing it and making it his life. He himself did not fish and regarded pleasure boats as he might model airplanes. To set off upon a finite expanse of water with no destination other than, ultimately, the dock from which one had set out seemed childish to a man who had spent fifteen years in the navy going into harm's way in Oriental waters, engaging in battles he never spoke of. It was the isolation and peace, the distance from the normal ways of men—for how did most human lives differ from the pointless excursions of pleasure boats?—and the chance for what he would have been embarrassed to call "contemplation" that attracted him to the North Woods. Withdrawal from urban surroundings had been further occasioned by estrangement from his wife, who it turned out had been faithful only in her fashion while he served his country.

A year or two after his return, they informally separated. She did not want a civil divorce, and Primero, a Catholic, had reacted with shock to the suggestion that he seek an annulment of his marriage. While it had not taken death to separate him and his wife, in his heart of hearts he remained her husband and thought of himself as still serving in foreign parts, away from her because of the demands of defending civilization and democracy. The country he had served disappointed him now, and in the North Woods it was possible to think that it was still the country he had joined the navy to preserve and protect.

When he received an offer for his resort, he succumbed but immediately built another and then another until he had a list of people for whom he had agreed to design and build resorts. He lived in the penthouse of one of the condominiums that he had built, but for much of the year he enjoyed the quiet and isolation of a monk in the north. He had a study in his apartment and he was electronically in touch with the wider world, so he spent as much time at Lake Constance as he could.

His house in Minneapolis also overlooked a lake, Lake of the Isles. That was the house from which his wife had fled. It was there that his Newman collection was kept, with Waldo Hermes occupying what had once been the servants' quarters over the garage.

When Primero traveled, it was as often as not in search of additions to his remarkable library rather than on business. Investments, where he proved to have the Midas touch, had multiplied many times over the fortune he had amassed as a builder of resorts. There were no living children from his marriage, so he collected books on the assumption that he would leave them, eventually, to someone else. That someone else proved to be Notre Dame.

On a visit to the campus he had met Greg Whelan, a canny archivist who knew and loved Newman. The addition of his Newman Collection to the Notre Dame library's holdings became attractive to Primero, and he liked the phlegmatic self-effacement of Greg Whelan in the university Archives. He also liked the suggestion of duplicating his catalog at Notre Dame so that the eventual transfer of the books would go smoothly. And then one day Hermes told him that the original pamphlet edition of the *Apologia Pro Vita Sua* was missing.

"I noticed it just two days ago," the luxuriantly bearded curator Waldo Hermes said. His eyes never left Primero's face, as if he were tracking the effect of this loss on his employer. "But I don't know how long it may have been missing."

"Has anyone asked to see it?"

Knowledgeable scholars had heard of Primero's private collection, and he had authorized Hermes to respond with discretion to requests to visit and peruse the Newman books and papers.

"I have studied the list of visitors."

But no one had asked to see the *Apologia* pamphlets. Of course anyone who had access to the catalog would know what was in the collection.

"I am making a thorough inventory to make sure nothing else is missing."

There was. A presentation copy of the first book edition of the *Apologia Pro Vita Sua*. A first edition of the *Grammar of Assent*.

Primero wished that Waldo would show more despondency at the loss. Since he was responsible, some measure of blame must inevitably attach to him. The question was, how much blame? It would of course occur to anyone that Waldo himself might have removed the missing items from the collection, but that was not an accusation Primero could bring himself to make. He telephoned Philip Knight on the advice of a fellow collector.

When the Knights arrived at the house by the Lake of the Isles, Philip talked with Primero while Roger renewed acquaintance with Waldo Hermes.

"And you live right here among these treasures?" Roger asked the custodian.

"I am seldom out of the house. When I'm not down here, I am in my rooms over the garage."

The security of the house ruled out a break-in and theft. Those who had visited the library seemed unlikely suspects.

"I think Mr. Primero thinks *I* took them," Waldo Hermes said. "Why would I? It's almost as if I own them now. Sell them and thus lose them? Never."

A theft without a suspect, or so it had seemed. When Hermes showed Roger the elaborate security arrangements in the house, not even the curator's defective hearing would have enabled anyone to enter unnoticed. Hermes set off the alarm to prove the point, and Primero and Phil rushed into the library. Primero seemed disappointed that it was only a false alarm.

"Who has keys to the house?" Roger asked.

Only Primero, Hermes, and his estranged wife, Bianca. Neither man had ever been separated from his keys.

The obvious explanation occurred to Roger almost immediately. "Where does your wife live?"

"She travels tirelessly."

"But she has an address."

Mrs. Primero lived in a high-rise apartment in Highland village, in the same condominium as Joseph, in a section of Saint Paul just across the Ford Bridge from the loveliest part of Minneapolis, Minnehaha Park. Here the creek, which began far off at Lake Minnetonka and was punctuated by the chain of city lakes through which it passed, spilled over the falls and continued to the river.

"How long has it been since she lived here?"

Primero knew to the day. Roger and Phil called on Bianca Primero, who was in her apartment between cruises. She was a willowy woman with golden hair; bright, mean eyes; and a smile that seemed to have come with her toothpaste. Her apartment was furnished in a modern impersonal style—the furniture consisting of cushions on steel frames, the rug in the living room looking as if it had been made from the hide of polar bears, the pictures on the wall outrageous denials that art imitates nature. There were no books in evidence, other than one shelf filled with travel guides and cruise brochures.

Bianca was an imposing woman, and at first, even at second, glance it was hard to believe that she was the same age as her husband. All the lesser surgical arts had been enlisted to stave off the effects of time on her flesh. The skin of her face was taut, any sag beneath her jaw had been removed. The general smoothness of her countenance, lightly brushed with cosmetics, and the glistening blue eyes framed by darkened lashes artfully suggested a woman in her late twenties, decades having been skimmed away. But it was a face that needed to be seen in flattering light.

When she stepped dramatically backward into her apartment after opening the door to the Knights, she might have been on a stage with carefully selected lighting.

53

"So you are the detectives."

"It's good of you to see us."

"It would be difficult not to," she said, looking significantly at Roger, who laughed at this allusion to his avoirdupois.

"I may be seen through but never overlooked."

Roger was given the couch after being steered away from a divan their hostess apparently thought inadequate to the task of supporting him.

"Now what is all this about Joseph's toys?"

Phil let Roger explain about the missing items. "As you must know, your husband's collection contains priceless items."

"Believe me, I know."

"Your husband has asked us to locate the missing materials."

Her elongated nails were blood red and their length made extracting a cigarette from a package difficult. When she had managed it, Phil rose to light it for her. She looked up at him through a cloud of exhaled smoke. "Joseph thinks I am responsible for the theft."

"Are you?"

"If I had my way, all that mildewed mumbo jumbo would go there." A long nail pointed to the fireplace. "Have you any idea what it is like to be married to a man who made a fortune in business but wants to pretend he is a scholar?"

"He hired us to look into the theft," Phil said, regaining his seat.

"And so you have come here."

"Do you have any idea who might have done it?"

She made a gesture with the hand that held the cigarette and ashes scattered over the rug. "Joseph himself could have done it."

"Joseph!"

"To get my attention. To bring about this visit. To annoy me. But he knows I will never again live in that library he has turned our house into."

54

"You don't share his interests?" Phil asked.

"My interest in books is probably on the same level as your own. Look around and you will see how different a setting I have made for myself. Only one small shelf of travel books."

"What about Waldo Hermes?" Roger asked.

"The hairy ape? He was the last straw. Imagine having a live-in librarian in your home."

No need to admit it to Roger, but Phil felt sympathy with the woman. She had her troubles. She and her husband had money; she wanted a life of leisure, travel, diversion. Not the wickedest of goals. Wasn't the collecting of priceless books self-indulgence of another kind? Why couldn't the Primeros compromise?

Bianca sighed. "Joseph must be devastated." She drew on her cigarette. "Those books are his children."

"I wonder who the kidnapper is," Phil said. "Any ideas?"

"You must know that Joseph and I have not lived together for years."

There was in her manner the suggestion that she was holding back something she might have told them.

Phil might have been flattered when Primero vetoed notifying the police. "I don't want publicity. I have every confidence in your ability to retrieve what has been taken."

"Is your library insured?"

Incredibly, it was not. "No money could compensate for the loss of the collection. I could not replace it. I entrust it to Providence."

"God permits evil to happen," Roger said.

Primero nodded, as if this was an endorsement of his views.

Phil advised Primero to change the locks on the doors of the Lake of the Isles home. Primero understood immediately and clearly accepted the implied accusation. Roger and Philip flew home first class to Chicago and took a commuter to South Bend. Phil had the sense of being toyed with. He had grown skeptical that a theft had occurred, a real theft.

"Can a wife steal from her husband?"

"It doesn't matter if he chooses not to bring in the police."

The day after their return, Roger gave Father Carmody a report of what had transpired in the Twin Cities.

"A woman scorned?" Father Carmody asked.

"Both Primeros said they had no children."

"None living," the priest said.

"Ah."

A son had died while Joseph was in the navy. Roger had the sense that they blamed one another for the loss. It seemed significant that she had referred to his books as her husband's children.

"He never got over it," the priest said. "Neither of them did."

9 ➤ A MYSTERIOUS PACKAGE AR-
rived at the Notre Dame Archives, brought
by Federal Express, and Greg Whelan signed for it. What is more
enticing than a newly arrived package, its contents undisclosed and
mysterious? Greg lifted the cardboard container in his hands as on
a scale; it was not light though not as heavy as he might have
wished, whatever it contained. He shook it, carefully, but no sound
fed his excited imagination. He got up from his desk and closed the
door of his office.

The sender was Primcro and although the package was not
addressed to him, simply to "Archives, Notre Dame, Indiana." Greg
worked in the Archives. He was, in fact, assistant director, but this
was a title held by several others as well. One of the sacred perks of
the director was to open or supervise the opening of any such package as this, and Wendy was rightly jealous of her prerogatives. As it
happened she was at the moment enjoying a long lunch in the University Club, trying to get a clearer picture of the future location of
the Archives from an enigmatic administrator. In the circumstances, it seemed to Greg Whelan that he had not only a right but
an obligation to open the package.

When he had done so, slowly, following the instructions on the
colorful container, and got his first glimpse of the contents, he rose
as if in reverence. Was it possible? He slid the ancient pages from
the container onto his desk, and there before his eyes were holograph letters written by Cardinal Newman himself. More accurately

the drafts of which fair copies had been sent. Without touching them, using the eraser ends of several pencils as instruments, he arranged them on his desk and stared down reverently at the handwriting of John Henry Cardinal Newman. It was a breathless moment. He was suddenly filled with that feeling captured in the scholastic maxim *bonum est diffusivum sui*. He wanted to share the moment, let other eyes than his own enjoy the vision of this treasure that had dropped unexpectedly from the sky. A fellow worker in the Archives? He shook the thought away as he reached for the phone. Who better than Roger Knight could appreciate what had arrived at the Archives?

Roger did not answer his office phone, and Greg chose not to leave a recorded message. He called the apartment of the Knight brothers and was told by Philip that Roger was on campus. Despite the difficulty with which he got around, Roger could be anywhere. And then, scarcely believing his ears, he heard Roger's voice outside his door. He sprang across the office and pulled open his door, startling Roger Knight who was about to knock.

"I have been trying to reach you. Come in, come in."

Inside, with the door closed, Greg led his visitor to his own desk chair, the only one remotely capable of containing the Huneker Chair of Catholic Studies. Roger settled into the chair, by stages, and then looked expectantly at Greg. The archivist pointed wordlessly at what lay upon his desk, and soon Roger was leaning over them. He did touch one of the letters, as one might touch a first-class relic. Then he looked up at Greg and spoke softly. "How did you come into possession of these?"

Greg handed him the FedEx envelope in which the items had arrived. This was not at all the reaction he had hoped for. Roger studied the package. He put a pudgy index finger on the sender's name, Primero. Just Primero. But the address was in Highland Village, Saint Paul.

"These are from the Primero Collection, Greg."

"Why would he have sent these now?"

"Greg, he has reported a theft."

Greg reacted as to a blasphemy. Roger promised him a full account. For the present, he suggested that Greg record the reception of the package and itemize its contents, then leave it on Wendy's desk. Meanwhile the two of them would go off and ponder the mystery.

Roger, Greg learned, had been with Phil to Minneapolis, summoned by Primero in their guise as detectives, where they had been told of missing items from the Primero Collection.

"He suspects Waldo Hermes."

Greg found this preposterous and said so. He had been working closely, if electronically, with Waldo Hermes ever since the decision had been made by Primero that the eventual destination of his Newman Collection was the Notre Dame Archives. Greg had recognized in Waldo the essential mark of the custodian of treasures amassed by another but destined for the common good. Daily traffic with such priceless collectibles strengthened the instinctive belief that they belonged to everyone, not to one alone. They were part of the common patrimony destined to be available, in principle, to all. From patron, to private collector, to museum or archive—that was the trajectory described by items destined to play a role in the common culture. To be a custodian was to be a trustee of the race, present and future; and in his dealings with Waldo Hermes, Greg Whelan had recognized a kindred spirit. To steal items in one's care was tantamount to seeking to appropriate the common air that all must breathe. Theft was unthinkable. Theft suggested that the common could be private property. The Maecenas, the private collector, eventually came to realize this himself. But for the custodian it was a self-evident principle.

"Of course this can hardly be regarded as theft if someone sent them to their intended eventual destination."

"It seems to have been Mrs. Primero who sent them."

"Even so."

Greg was glad that it was Roger he had informed of the receipt of these priceless items. Whatever shenanigans in Minneapolis explained the surprising and premature transfer of these items from the Primero Collection, it was important that the university and the Archives—as well as his own reputation—not be tainted.

"I think I understand what happened," Roger said.

"Which is?"

"I want to talk to my brother first."

"It seems a kind of joke."

"Yes, but on whom?"

After Roger left, Greg kept the treasure for a time, once more laying out on his desk the letters written in a hand familiar to the archivist because he had seen so many reproductions of it. But he had never before seen an actual holograph, the very page the cardinal had had before him and on which he had formed those inky words, fully legible now a century and a half later. These of course were first drafts, fair copies of which would have been made and posted. The amount of time spent on correspondence then, the need to draft and then copy, involved much labor-intensive effort. In an age when the mere tapping of fingers sufficed to bring upon the monitor a string of words, the whole corrigible in a quince, the approved version printed out simply by pressing a key, the method Newman and others had to use seemed at once both primitive and more personal. How much more thoughtful a letter must have have been under those circumstances than when one's fingers flew across the keys and then flashed the result across the telephone wires. Multiple exchanges between E-mail correspondents could take place in the course of a few minutes. It was doubtful that any such message would retain any literary interest. The process had become merely functional. But a nineteenth-century letter was a work of art, roughed out first and then polished, the better to express the thought and feeling of its author. Newman had dedicated hours of each day to his correspondence. And here on Greg Whelan's desk were a few items of the mountain of letters Newman had written, the printed volumes of which marched across the library shelves.

One of the letters was to Orestes Brownson, on the occasion of his negative review of *An Essay on the Development of Christian Doctrine;* there were several to an editor in Ireland. But there were two letters that particularly fascinated Whelan, the first addressed to Gerard Manley Hopkins.

Hopkins was one of those who had become a Roman Catholic under the influence of Newman and then entered the Jesuit order, ultimately assigned to teach in Dublin where some of his most anguished poems had been penned. Newman's letter to the young man antedated all that of course, and neither correspondent could have known what lay ahead. Whelan had a sudden image of the condition of man, whether by thought or deed or writing, pushing against the membrane of the present in search of a glimpse of what the future held, the future that soon enveloped one by becoming the present and pointing beyond itself to a further future. At whatever pace one lived—the seemingly glacial pace of the nineteenth-century correspondent or the computer speed of the present—the image was fundamentally the same. We move like a cursor across the page of time. . . .

Greg Whelan felt an impulse to write that down. Once he had

longed to be a poet, but he had never succeeded in separating himself from the academic world. Having gained a doctorate in English, his speech impairment, in the contemporary phrase—he stuttered—had precluded employment. Interview after interview ended with Greg trying to stammer an answer to a question asked by a member of the interviewing committee. He had gone to law school in the mad hope that therapy and determination would loosen his tongue so that he might become a master of forensic oratory. But he was as incapable of public speech at the end of law school as he had been in the beginning. In near despair he had trained as a librarian and, as if God had intended it all along, was hired as an archivist at Notre Dame. Here he had been ever since, his contentment with his lot immeasurably increased when Roger Knight was appointed Huneker Chair of Catholic Studies. The two men became friends, linked by many intellectual interests. But there still lurked in the breast of Gregory Whelan the ambition to be a poet. And here was a letter addressed by Newman to one of Greg's favorite poets.

Another letter was to Anthony Trollope, written in August 1875, concerning the depiction of the Catholic priest, Father Barham, in *The Way We Live Now*. Newman had much praise for the novel but took umbrage at charges against the priesthood that he himself had faced from Charles Kingsley and had answered in the *Apologia*. The novel was one in which Trollope lamented the conditions of the time, and with few exceptions, the characters represented the decline of standards of morality as well as common courtesy. Newman acknowledged that but hoped that Trollope would reconsider his view that the Roman clergy were shady types for whom the end justified the means.

How he envied Waldo Hermes, who had access to such items as

these. Once he had considered Waldo a threat to his own job, but when Waldo came to campus with Primero, that fear was lifted.

Joseph Primero had brought his archivist to campus with him, and Wendy had arranged a meeting between the benefactor and a man named Hannan in the Office of Notre Dame Development. The topic was the proposed building that would house the Primero Collection. It was this that had filled Greg Whelan with apprehension. He was sure that the university would parlay the need for an adequate setting for Primero's books into a new building large enough to accommodate the entire university archival holdings. And what if Waldo Hermes was included in the package?

Whelan's speech impediment would have made him useless at the meeting, even if he had been asked, as he had not. How easy it was to imagine Wendy offering him up in sacrifice for the generous gift of Joseph Primero. Even if Hermes was brought in simply to care for the Primero things and Whelan retained for other lesser work in the Archives, it would be the dashing of hopes that had been nurtured for years.

"My fate is in the balance," Whelan had said to Roger Knight at the time. They were lunching in the University Club, whose acoustics had the properties of Saint Paul's in London, a whisper audible across the room, a shout all but inaudible across the table. Greg's stammer mysteriously left him whenever he conversed with Roger Knight, as if the professor's colossal weight balanced out his own impediment.

"How so?"

"Primero's custodian could be part of the deal."

"That would be cruel."

"But it would make sense. He has been working with the collection for years. First hand."

"But you expected to have it delivered into your hands."

"No one promised me that."

The morality of institutions is a topic worthy of inquiry. What would be a vice in an individual becomes accepted institutional practice. For a scholar to call attention to his own achievements, tout and trumpet them to the world, would be a cause for embarrassment among his colleagues, a clear flaw of character. But universities have huge bureaucracies dedicated to just such trumpeting. The faculty is required to send in lists of grants, publications, talks and presentations, and these are collectively shouted to the four winds by the university's Office of Public Relations and Information. Was it the public as opposed to private that was thought to justify such vanity?

A theory that Roger had encountered among colleagues who shared his own surprise at the university's practice of publicizing the achievements of its faculty was that this is the mark of an institution on the rise, one without confidence in its own worth. Why should it be taken almost as a surprise that members of the faculty wrote, that they were invited here and there because of what they knew? It was like the applause that sometimes burst out at the end of transatlantic flights, the passengers cheering for the successful landing. But the age of Lindbergh had long since passed. Arriving at its destination should not be a cause for surprise in an airliner. So too, a productive faculty should be a given, understood, not drawn attention to as if it were a prodigy.

"Do you know the essay called 'The Vice of Gambling and the Virtue of Insurance'?" Wyser in Philosophy had once asked Roger.

"I must read it."

"The title is the best thing about it. But you see the analogy."

64

"Individual vices are institutional virtues?"

"Not much of a title."

A feature of this institutional practice was that it led to a kind of boredom with the current faculty and a tendency to be disproportionately impressed by a scholar whose achievements had hitherto been unknown. He must be hired!

Greg listened to Roger, enjoying his giant friend's wit and wisdom even if he doubted its consolations would survive their lunch. Afterward Roger gave him a ride in his golf cart back to the library. Waldo Hermes was waiting for him in his office. The big question was: Would he or would he not stutter. Hermes turned from the window that gave a panoramic view of the northern Indiana countryside.

"Everything is so flat."

"That is how it struck me at first. You get used to it." He hadn't stuttered.

"I don't think I could."

"What will you do when the Primero Collection is brought here?"

Hermes looked like a shy animal peering from the underbrush. "That isn't going to happen tomorrow, you know."

"But when it does?"

"How old do you think I am?"

There were flecks of gray in the facial hair, but atop Hermes's head the luxuriant growth showed no streaks of silver.

"About my age?"

"Are you fifty-eight?"

"Are you?"

The eyes twinkled through the underbrush. "On my next birthday. So I am in my fifty-eighth year."

"I would never have guessed."

"In any case, I will at last be in a position to concentrate on my own collection." He coughed. "Or my soul."

"You're a collector."

"In a modest way. I could become immodest in retirement. Mr. Primero has provided me with a very handsome retirement package."

All this was music to Greg Whelan's ears. The threat to his own custody of the Primero papers once arrived at Notre Dame was lifted. Every barrier to the two curators becoming real friends had been removed.

"I envy you," Greg lied. "Retirement" as a word was in the same class as "terminal illness" so far as he was concerned. Like an eminent predecessor when the library was new, Greg Whelan would have been content to be found at his desk some Monday morning, gone to his reward without a fuss.

Memories of Waldo Hermes's visit came to him now with the Newman letters before him. How reluctant he felt to surrender them. Almost without thinking, as if to avoid catching the eye of conscience in the mirror of the moment, Greg slipped the letters under his desk blotter. They were far safer there than they would be lying on the director's desk awaiting her return. He would make photocopies, of course, but for now he wanted to keep these treasures to himself.

10 WITH NANCY BEATTY ON THE seat beside him, Roger Knight maneuvered his golf cart along the campus walks in the direction of the Grotto. Nancy had wanted to hear about the trip to Minneapolis, given the anxiety the absence of the Knight brothers had caused her, and Roger suggested an excursion in his cart to the community cemetery. After a stop at the Grotto, where Roger somewhat apologetically said his prayers without getting out of the golf cart, they headed up the road toward Saint Mary's under the great trees that formed a canopy above them.

"Larry was out of town too," she said. "He still is."

"Oh?"

"A wrinkle has arisen about where our wedding will take place."

And she told Roger the story as she had gotten it from Larry. Of course undergraduates fall in love, and often; but from time to time a couple was formed that was destined to last a lifetime. Apparently Larry had thought he and the girl he was going with were such a couple. He'd proposed, she'd accepted, they'd agreed that they would marry three years after graduation.

"They actually scheduled a date at Sacred Heart?"

"June 17, 2002."

"That's when you're getting married!"

"In order that we might take advantage of the reservation at the Basilica."

"Larry had more foresight than he knew."

"Not quite. The date has already been claimed by his old girl-friend. Larry is furious and went to Minneapolis to beg her to get married somewhere else. He was sure we had the better claim on June 17."

The situation could be amusing only to those not involved in it, and Roger felt involved because of his friendship with Nancy and Larry. What would be the likelihood that two people who had decided on their wedding date would, when they broke up and formed new alliances, both decide to marry on that very date? Surely Larry had been justified in thinking the date was free. Just as surely the former fiancée had been justified in thinking the same.

"That must have been an interesting encounter."

"Not too interesting, I hope."

Roger stirred on the seat and lifted his brows. He drove the slow-moving cart as if he were at the wheel of a race car at Le Mans, two hands gripping the wheel, never looking anywhere but straight ahead where any contingency might suddenly confront him.

"How so?"

"He was engaged to her, you know."

"But she's engaged to someone else now."

"I know." Nancy's voice carried a little thread of worry. "But he's got a low boiling point."

"When will Larry return?"

"The firm that hired him wants him to spend some time there, and he agreed to stay over. He called this morning to tell me all about it."

"Will the girl concede the date to you and Larry?"

"She hasn't yet. But Larry hasn't given up hope. Now that he will be in Minneapolis a few days, he thinks he can persuade her."

"Let's hope so."

"I don't like him seeing her that much."

"About their different weddings!"

"A girl has a right to be foolish once in a while."

"A duty I should say. But I wouldn't worry about Larry."

"What, me worry?" She looked at him cross-eyed.

"Phil has gone back to Minneapolis. Maybe they can get together."

This was at Roger's suggestion. Greg Whelan had checked the inventory of the Primero Collection he had on his computer and was surprised to find that the Newman letters sent to the Archives were not listed.

"I was as surprised as I was delighted," he told Roger. "I suppose I should log them in here. Maybe that was the intention."

"You haven't yet?"

Greg look shamefaced. He lifted his desk blotter, giving Roger a glimpse of the letters as if they were postcards sold along the Seine.

"They're still a secret. Wendy has been so busy, I haven't told her yet. Meanwhile . . ." He lifted a corner of the desk blotter and sighed.

Phil's excuse for going to Minneapolis was to get a full and accurate list of the missing items. But the point was to speak with Waldo. Primero had suspected Waldo when the theft occurred, but who wouldn't? But the case against it being Waldo was stronger than the affirmative case. Unless of course it turned out that he had intended to sell the missing memorabilia.

They had arrived at their destination, and Roger brought the golf cart across the gravelly little arc that served as a parking lot for visitors to the community cemetery. Then began the major operation of getting unbuckled and out of the cart.

"We must visit the grave of Father Sorin."

But on the way to the grave of the founder of Notre Dame, Roger was distracted by crosses bearing the names of other figures from the university's past.

"Father Zahm!" he cried, and for a moment he seemed about to sink to his knees. "The great scientist. The friend of Teddy Roosevelt. He wrote a book on women in science. Most important of all, we owe the Dante Collection to him."

How could Father Sorin compete with this?

11 WHEN HE WAS TOLD THAT A
Mrs. Primero was on the line, Dudley had to
make an effort to retain the authoritative aplomb that was an essential part of his office persona.

"Tell her I will call her back in ten minutes."

He got up and shut his office door and, once more behind his desk, took a cell phone from his briefcase and then sat for a moment, trying to rehearse the call he was about to make. It had been two weeks since he had spoken with Bianca, and that had been to tell her he would be out of town and unable to see her. It was stupid to put off the evil day when he would tell her it was all over, but he did not quite know how to break the news to her.

Early on in their relationship he had thought she would tire of him and everything would simply drift away, leaving little trace on either of their souls. But something had happened to their affair. At first he had been merely a diversion, a way to stave off the boredom that haunted Bianca. He had felt like someone sent to her from a male escort bureau and had little illusion that she had any real interest in him. He imagined himself to be one in a faceless series of mindless tumbles in the hay, the toy of an older woman of incredible yet oddly charming egocentricity. But her talk had been largely weary narratives of her trips and cruises. Any friends she had during the marriage from which she said she was on leave had been abandoned for the strangers she met on boats and in the far corners of the world, aged swingers like herself who made no real claim on her.

It had seemed so casual at first.

"Tell me all about yourself, Dud."

The nickname was both intimate and derisive. "You would find it all impossibly dull."

"Would I?" She lit an elongated cigarette and expelled a cloud of mentholated smoke. "Sometimes I envy you your scheduled day. Freedom is overrated."

A new Bianca emerged. The woman who had everything now realized she had nothing.

"Maybe you should go back to your husband."

"Do you think so?" She had turned to look at him.

"I really know nothing about it."

"No, you don't. But I have thought of it."

"Oh?" He tried to conceal his joy.

She drew on her cigarette. "Till recently that seemed a possibility."

Her tone was meaningful, and he felt both flattered and frightened. What there was between them was in the nature of things temporary, a finite affair, destined to be ended and probably sooner rather than later. He sat in silence, not wanting to encourage this mood.

"You're such a dud."

"Only nominally."

An odd prelude to her opening her arms and drawing her to him. He was very conscious of the lighted cigarette in the fingers of one of the hands behind his head. He reached for it and stubbed it out in the ashtray. She watched him do this, then lifted her lips to his.

Passion seemed the best postponement of any discussion of her mood.

He pushed these memories away. Now in his office, he punched her number on his cell phone. She answered immediately.

"Is that you?"

"Yes."

"How was your trip?"

He had to remind himself of his make-believe trip that had gained him a weekend with Dolores. "The usual thing."

"And what is that? Dudley, I want to hear all about it. Let's have dinner tonight."

"I'll make a reservation."

"Please don't. I want to cook for you."

He agreed. It would be the grand finale. A sentimental evening, remembering old times, the fun they'd had, and then he would explain to her how it was. There was no future for them. He couldn't mention the discrepancy in their ages, but the fact that she was a married woman was decisive enough. If she had intended to get divorced, she would have done so long ago. There must be advantages for her in remaining the legal wife of a man she could no longer abide but who himself seemed still hopelessly in love with Bianca. Or at least hopelessly committed to her. Divorce would never be proposed on his side. "He's very Catholic," Bianca had told Dudley, making a sour little face.

Well, if Bianca was married and no divorce was in prospect, there was no need to say that no amount of cosmetic surgery could erase the gap between their ages. And he would appeal to her better side. She must have one. He was a young man. It was time that he married. Should he tell her the whole truth, that he was now engaged to Dolores? I'll play it by ear, he told himself after he had parked his car and was heading for the door of Bianca's building.

The meal was a triumph. *Saltimbocca alla Romana,* with a sauce that was so succulent Dudley sopped it all up with garlic bread. The wine was a Barolo. It amazed him that Bianca could cook so well.

She dismissed his flattery. "Men are better cooks than women."

"Not this man and this woman."

"Have you ever tried?"

He shook his head. He knew what he thought of men who cooked and baked. "This has been a wonderful evening."

"My dear, the night is young."

"We have to talk, Bianca."

"What have we been doing since you got here?"

"About us."

He had helped her carry things into the kitchen, where she rinsed dishes and put them in the washer as if she were determined to continue in her role. This whole domestic persona was new to Dudley. She turned to him and her carefully shaped brows formed crescents above her eyes. "You sound serious."

"Let's sit down."

She permitted him to lead her to the couch. She sat at the far end, facing him. "I won't let you steal my thunder, sweetheart. The whole point of this evening was to have the proper setting for my announcement."

"Announcement?"

She smiled tenderly, dipping her head and peering at him. "I have decided to ask Joseph for a divorce."

Dudley sat in stunned silence.

"I have felt your discontent with the way things have been. And you're right. Oh, I confess it. At first I thought of you as a diversion. A handsome, intelligent, affectionate diversion, but nothing more. It has long since passed the point where I can deceive myself that this is the case."

"Bianca . . ."

She held up her hand. "I have the floor. It broke my heart when you would complain of the impermanence of our arrangement."

Had he ever complained of that?

"I will not come between a man and his wife."

"But, darling, you already have. The deed is done. And now I am prepared to accept the logical conclusion. Away with impermanence; I intend to be free and then . . ."

"Will he grant you a divorce?"

"Ha. How can he stop me?"

"But what would be your reason?"

"Marital infidelity."

"Joseph?" Had Primero been driven to a compensatory affair?

"No, my own. Ours. If he should make any trouble, I will make public our love and our intention to marry."

"Is this a proposal?" he asked, in a strangled effort to be jocular. "Bianca, you can't just make such decisions for other people."

"What do you mean?"

"That I don't want you to get a divorce."

"You wily thing." She smiled a naughty smile. "Do you prefer me in the illicit mode?"

He grasped at this as a check on her plans, if not a way out. "Why change such a good thing?"

She was touched. She slithered toward him on the couch, and he took her in his arms as the means of preventing her from going on with her absurd plans. Did she seriously think that he would marry her?

"You want a mistress rather than a wife."

"I want you just the way you are."

The evening had been anything but what he had intended when he drove to Bianca's apartment. But then it had not been what she had intended either. They remained mistress and gigolo, and in an odd way that seemed an achievement.

But when he left, she said something that made it clear that she had known what she was forestalling when she announced her intention to get a divorce.

"Give little Dolores my best."

"Dolores?"

"Your assistant, isn't she?"

On the drive to his own place he wondered if her talk about getting a divorce was merely an ad hoc defense against what she feared he would say. What had he told her of Dolores that had prompted that final exchange?

WHEN DOLORES GOT A CALL
from Bianca Primero asking her to lunch, she
had no idea who she was. "I'm an old friend of Dudley's." Something about the way the woman said this both annoyed Dolores and
excited her curiosity. She allowed herself to be coaxed, but after she
accepted she did not tell Dudley. She had the feeling he would tell
her not to go.

The selection of Dayton's Tea Room might have been meant as
ironic, but Dolores didn't mind. She would have gone to McDonald's to find out who Bianca Primero was.

She was a surprise, an older woman, nice as pie at first. Dolores
might have been having lunch with an aunt.

"It was wise not to tell Dudley," Bianca said after several minutes of idle back and forth chatter.

"How do you know I didn't?"

"Because you're here." She lit a cigarette in an elaborate ritual,
bringing the manager on the run.

"You can't smoke here, ma'am! This is a smoke-free restaurant."

"Even in the kitchen?" She blew smoke at him and then tapped
the cigarette out in her bread plate. She handed it to the manager.
He took it, paused, tried to smile, turned and left. "Ass."

"Would you rather go somewhere else?" Dolores asked.

"I will certainly never come back here. Have you ever been here
before?"

"No."

"It is a favorite haunt of young matrons, I'm told. Perhaps you will see a lot of it in the future."

"Perhaps."

"So what has Dudley told you of me?"

"What would he tell me?"

"How we met for instance." Bianca smiled. "One Saturday morning in Highland Village, in a gallery. He was admiring a sentimental beach scene, mother with children, soft blues and yellows and whites."

"No, he didn't tell me. Why would he?"

"I bought the picture."

"Why are you telling me this?"

"Oh, come now. Why are we having lunch together? It's the passing of the baton, is it not? I don't mean to be crude. Do you find me old?"

"You look marvelous."

And she did. Dolores had been studying the woman across from her. That she was older than Dudley was clear, but she certainly was not *old*. Her suggestion was that Dudley had come under her spell, but perhaps it was the other way around. Acting the good sport, might be just that for Bianca Primero.

"Why, thank you." But then she seemed to wonder if the remark had another significance. There was a not quite visible change in her manner. "You do not find me too old for Dudley?"

Dolores's breath caught at the implication of the remark. "Don't you?"

"The important thing is that he does not. I suppose he has told you that everything is over between us?" She smiled a radiant smile. "I authorized him to tell you that. I didn't tell him I would deny it, but then he doesn't know we're meeting, does he?"

"I will tell him everything." She could hardly wait to talk with him about this strange lunch and stranger conversation.

"Lunch with his old flame?"

"Is that how you think of yourself?"

"Isn't that how you think of me."

"I don't know what to think of you. I had never heard of you until you called. What was the purpose of asking me to lunch?"

"Well, I thought I might offer to share Dudley with you if he should marry you."

Dolores just stared at the woman.

"That doesn't appeal to you?"

"It's absurd."

"Then again Dudley and I might marry. In that case I would be less broad-minded."

"Don't you have a husband?"

"Yes. But I could have another."

Dolores had thought of herself as a woman of the world—she was successful in her work, in charge of her life—but she felt reduced to gawky girlhood by this woman in whom the normal effects of age had been surgically removed. She sensed a wickedness in Bianca she had never before encountered. It was malicious and pointless. She was suggesting that Dudley had been her lover but she did not speak of love. Had Dudley been her amusement? Now she was annoyed by the prospect of losing him.

But it was her own position that Dolores was forced to consider. She had been asked to lunch by an older woman who effectively claimed to have been Dudley's mistress. But it was the woman, not Dudley, she despised. Her womanly impulse to forgive Dudley almost surprised her. Of course this woman would lie and pretend that what had been still went on, but she was desperate. For her

Dolores felt no forgiveness. It seemed obvious to Dolores that, if anything had gone on between them, Bianca had seduced Dudley. Dolores felt suddenly full of the wisdom that comes from being a woman. What children men are, and how easily they are led about. And how easily a woman can abuse the power she has over them.

Dolores barely touched what she had ordered and insisted on separate checks. She would take nothing from this woman.

"You must be dying for a smoke." It seemed a way to end it.

"Where there's smoke . . ." Bianca lifted her brows and Dolores half expected her to waggle them, like Groucho. She was glad to make her escape.

13   "OH, MY GOD," DUDLEY CRIED,
when Dolores told him about the lunch, as
she had promised Bianca she would.

"She is a pathetic creature."

"She is evil. You should never have agreed to see her."

"I had to see her."

He looked at her. "Yes, I suppose you did. But never see her
again, she means to destroy us."

"How on earth could she do that?"

He fell silent and took her hand. "Of course she couldn't. You're
right." He tried to take her in his arms.

"Let me catch my breath."

It was an excuse not a reason, and they both knew it. Dolores
looked at him in silence before finally speaking. "Dudley, you let
me think that you were unattached."

"Unattached?"

"Not emotionally committed to someone else."

"What did Bianca say?"

"The question is, Why didn't I hear it from you?"

He stepped back and nodded. "You're right. I was wrong not to,
but I thought I was unattached, as you put it."

"More like detached?"

"It is true that I was once close to Mrs. Primero . . ."

"Mrs. Primero! Is that how you address her?"

He tried a little laugh, not as unsuccessfully as he had feared. "The perks of age."

"Is she as old as she must be?"

"Dolores, what are you getting at?"

"That you've been involved in a long-term affair with Bianca Primero."

"Do you really believe that?"

"It's not true?"

"Not in the way you put it, no. Dolores, whatever it was, it's all over. I never claimed to be a monk, did I? Do you think I could be interested in anyone but you now? The past is the past. Did I have a fit when I learned that you had been engaged to marry before? How did I take it when your discarded fiancé came strutting into our life . . . ?"

"Dudley, it is hardly the same thing."

But he could see that the moral imbalance between them was being corrected. He moved close to her but did not attempt to take her in his arms. "The point, Dolores, is now. I have not lived the life of an altar boy. But wouldn't it have been odd if I had told you about Mrs. Primero? Falling in love is like general absolution, Dolores. It sweeps away the past."

She let him take her in his arms then, and he held her close. He almost trembled with relief.

He was of course in a dilemma of his own making. He should have cast Bianca off long ago, chalking it up to experience. For that matter, why hadn't she tired of him? Even now, when he seemed more enmeshed in her web than ever, he could not believe that she really cared for him. Divorce Primero and marry him? That was just a play in the game whose stakes had become more interesting when Bianca had somehow learned of Dolores. Amy?

How sweet she would find it to triumph over a young and beautiful woman.

It had been a mistake to suggest to Dolores that Bianca meant to destroy them. He must diminish her importance not increase it. She was a youthful indiscretion, that was his story. But then why was she asking his fiancée to lunch?

The point where a simple solution was possible had long since passed. Before Dolores, he could have broken away and there would have been nothing Bianca could have done to hurt him. Tell a story of being betrayed by Dudley Fyte to the senior partners of Kunert and Skye? The suspicion might have been a feather in his cap to the old roués on the corner offices. Now she could undermine his engagement to Dolores.

It was an added annoyance that Larry Morton was still in town. Even if he'd left, he would be returning to join a firm even more prestigious than Kunert and Skye. Dudley did not like the way Dolores acted with Larry. An easy camaraderie had been reestablished, seemingly a return to their undergraduate days. But it was then that they had become engaged and had reserved a date for their wedding at Sacred Heart.

"I wonder about taking that date," Dudley said.

"Why! I am still battling for it."

"It could be a jinx."

"You don't believe that."

Her hand on his arm, her shoulder against him, dismissed the subject. But he didn't like feeling like a substitute sent in to take the place of Larry Morton at Dolores's side before the altar of the basilica. Had Larry told her of seeing him with Bianca?

It had been in a bar crowded with commuters yet to flee for their trains. Bianca was loving the crushed excitement of the place, prelude to their attending a play he did not want to see. His times with Bianca had become command performances, invitations he did not dare refuse, although any menace was covered over by her increasingly affectionate manner. She clung to him in the bar and looked up at him with eager, possessive eyes. And then, suddenly, there was Larry Morton next to them. Dudley greeted him quickly, a preemptive strike.

"Dudley, how are you?" Larry was holding his glass high, out of range of elbows. He looked at Bianca, then at Dudley, waiting for an introduction. He seemed to have lost all urgency to push on through the crowd.

"I am Bianca Primero." A long-nailed hand was extended to Larry.

"Larry Morton."

"One of your colleagues, darling?"

Morton looked even more closely at Bianca now. Darling? Dudley could have wrung her neck.

"Afraid not, sweetie pie." He winked at Larry. "We couldn't afford him."

"Have to get back to Dolores," Larry said, returning the wink.

"Dolores?" Bianca cried.

But she smiled at him, her eyes narrowed, her gaze inquisitive. Dudley tried not to follow Larry through the crowd. He would give anything to know if he really was with Dolores. A moral standoff? Betrothed couple out with former loves? But getting Bianca out of there was a more compelling objective.

Had Larry told Dolores and she'd remained silent? Dudley prepared a series of possible lies if confronted with the story. Bianca was supposed to be a folly of the past, not a present companion. What was he doing with her in a Loop bar? Could he counter by saying that Larry mentioned that she was with him? He throbbed with jealousy. Only the guilty are capable of unbridled moral indignation. He decided he would mention it to Dolores.

The occasion came when they were in his office, getting ready to go to the conference room where Dolores would explain the use of the combined database she had created for the firm. It was for this that she had been hired by Kunert and Skye, and though this had led to her job as assistant to Dudley Fyte, she was committed to complete it. And she had.

"I saw your friend Larry last night."

"Oh." Disinterest. She was arranging overheads in a folder.

"In a bar. O'Callaghans."

"Where's that?"

"On Michigan. It's close to where he works."

"What were you doing over there."

"Having a drink."

"That's what bars are for."

He was certain now that she did not know he had been with Bianca. But relief proved allusive. All that meant was that Larry hadn't told her yet.

There was an exclamation from the outer office, and then Amy looked in. "A huge package just arrived."

"How huge?" Dudley left Dolores and went into Amy's office. The package leaned against her desk. He saw the sender and immediately grabbed the top of the box. He carried it into his office and leaned it against the wall, with the address and sender toward the wall.

"What's that?" Dolores asked.

"God knows."

Amy stood in the doorway. "Aren't you going to open it. I'm dying to see what it is."

"Not now. Dolores has a presentation to make."

He felt that he was escaping when he took Dolores's arm and escorted her down the corridor to her waiting audience, junior partners, the hierarchy of Kunert and Skye. Dudley introduced her.

"I won't pretend to understand all this myself. The great point of having Dolores Torre with this firm is that you and I need not understand the arcane points of computerized legal research. But there are some things we have to learn if we are to profit from the system Dolores has put together."

The presentation was a model of clarity. Dolores spoke with authority but did not intimidate. Nor did she condescend. Her manner was matter-of-fact, assuming that these successful lawyers could grasp something as simple as tapping into a database that would make traditional ways of doing legal research seem primitive by comparison. Dolores had been working on this system ever since she had come to Kunert and Skye from West Publishing.

Once the advantages of the system were clear, she explained the relatively easy way of using it and then engaged in a colloquy with her pupils. It was a triumph. Dudley waited while Dolores received the plaudits of his colleagues, and then he took her to his office. Before he closed the door, Amy marched in. "Okay. Let's open it."

She went to the package and before Dudley could stop her, turned it around. In the upper corner, printed with magic marker, was the very legible name of the sender, Bianca Primero.

"Yes, Dudley," Dolores said, "open it. I'm as anxious as Amy."

He had no choice. It had become a public event. The paper covered a crate and within the crate was a painting, framed.

"Take it out, Dudley. Let's see it."

He gripped the top of the frame and began to lift it. When did he first know what picture it would be? Before it fully emerged from the crate, before Dolores and Amy had taken it and propped it against the wall so that they could all see the beach scene with mother and child in blues and yellows.

"It's lovely!" Amy cried.

"A little sentimental, perhaps." Dolores stood, one leg before the other, head lowered, hand to her chin, looking at the painting. She swung on Dudley. "But what memories it must bring back!"

Amy's presence made it difficult to prevent Dolores from going. She left rapidly, without a further word. After an awkward moment, Amy followed, closing the door after her.

Dudley leaned against the desk and gazed at the loathsome beach scene. This was the picture he had been inspecting in the Highland Village gallery the first time Bianca spoke to him. "Sentimental," she had said. Was sending the painting a sentimental gesture, or something else? Bianca had no intention of fading from the scene.

THE PAINTING HAD BEEN THE last straw. Dolores knew enough to guess the value of that painting. Just a little bauble from his mistress? But it was the painting's significance that seemed clear; Bianca Primero was making her claim on Dudley.

Dolores went rapidly down the hall, but before she could leave several people who had enjoyed her presentation stopped her to say so. All that already seemed months in the past. In the few minutes since, she felt that her whole life had become unglued. Everything Dudley had led her to believe about Bianca was false. Everything Bianca had told her seemed true.

So what was Dolores to do about all the detailed plans that had been made? Mrs. Torre was to fly into Chicago's O'Hare airport, and Dolores and Dudley would meet her there and rent a car for the trip to South Bend. These arrangements had been made weeks before. Mrs. Torre was understandably excited at the prospect of her daughter's marriage and intended to exercise her prerogative of making all the arrangements. That meant going to South Bend, talking with Father Rocca, making arrangements at The Morris Inn for the reception.

Dolores drove home and when she got there remembered absolutely nothing about the drive, her mind had been so full of the confusion brought on by Dudley's implied admission and the silly expression he'd worn when the painting arrived to mock everything he had been trying to say. There was a message from Larry on her answering machine, and she was about to dial the number he'd left when the phone rang. It was Dudley.

"That painting was a farewell gift, Dolores. Sayonara. It's over. That's what it meant."

"But why *that* painting?"

"God only knows."

"Not only God, Dudley. Bianca told me."

"Dolores . . ."

But she was in no mood to discuss it with him and finally he let her go. Then she called the number Larry had left.

"Just wanted to let you know I'm still in town. I've been asked to stay over another week."

"Will I see you?"

"I don't suppose you're free tonight."

"What did you have in mind?"

He had in mind a pub in Mendota with bar food—fatty, full of cholesterol, lethal.

"Sounds good."

Mendota was a historic little town on the banks of the Mississippi, now all but canopied by interstates and colonized by Saint Paul. Calling the bar a pub was a misnomer, but the food was as described. The place had been through many transformations. A wooden bar ran the length of the left wall, booths ringing what had once been a dance floor but over which tables were now scattered. And crowded. The popularity of such places is one of the minor mysteries of life. They took a booth. In a far corner, a piano, a trombone, and a saxophone evoked the songs of yesterday—several days before yesterday.

"So they asked you to stay in town for a few days? Can't wait to have you in the firm?"

"Dolores, I want to make one last claim on that reservation."

She looked at him and began to cry. Quietly. Biting on her lower lip. Ashamed of herself, but unable to stop. Larry put his hand on hers and had the good sense not to say anything. He fetched a handkerchief from his pocket with the other hand and gave it to her.

"I'm sorry."

"Tell me about it."

And, incredibly, she did. All of it. It helped some that Larry was not surprised.

"So it's all over."

"I don't know."

He hunched toward her but then the waitress skidded up and they ordered. Again he leaned toward her and again his hand closed over hers. "You must have noticed what I think of the guy, Dolores. The older woman? I saw her with him."

"You did?"

"I wouldn't have told you if you hadn't said what you've said. They were in a bar on Michigan."

"He said he saw you there."

Larry was surprised. "He was clearly shaken when he saw me. Dolores, none of this surprises me. That sounds smug and maybe it is, but I think you deserve someone a lot better than Dudley Fyte."

"The way he acted with you, Larry? That was not characteristic. You have to realize that he was jealous. I hadn't told him about us. He had no idea how impossible it would have been just to call the Basilica and make a reservation for a June wedding. I didn't have to explain that."

"What's to explain?"

She didn't try to explain that it established a kind of moral equivalence between Dudley and her. She had been engaged to marry; he had been involved with Bianca. Had her reaction to the arrival of the painting in Dudley's office been irrational? It could seem ridiculous in light of his plausible explanation of it as a farewell gift from Bianca Primero. And what was *she* doing telling Larry all about it as they sat in a bar in Mendota?

His hand was still on hers, and she left it there. Mostly, they said nothing, but the silence seemed more and more significant. Dolores remembered how it had been with Larry all those years ago when they were undergraduates at Notre Dame. It had been such a chaste relationship. Deciding to marry had been an aspect of that, a great promissory note that what they denied themselves now would be theirs in the future. Not saying too much was their only option now. He had been wonderfully sympathetic, but he had not pressed her to say things about Dudley she might regret. Dolores half envied him what she took to be the innocent simplicity of his own wedding plans. Perhaps she imagined it as just a repetition of what she and Larry had had. God knows her relationship with Dudley was not at all like that.

Larry took her home, took her to her door, kissed her on the cheek, and gave her a big hug. And that was it. Had she expected anything else?

Baring her heart to Larry had somehow reconciled her to Dudley. She accepted his explanation of the painting. Much of the sheen was gone from their relationship, but maybe it was the more solid for that. She did not cancel the trip to South Bend, telling herself that all doubts about Dudley and Mrs. Primero seemed resolved. On the way from O'Hare to South Bend, her mother chattered in the backseat of the rental car all ninety miles to campus, intent on enjoying every moment of Dolores's wedding preparations. They left her with the manager of The Morris Inn and went to keep their appointment with the rector of Sacred Heart Basilica.

"Of course you'll have to take a marriage preparation course," the priest said.

"Here!" Dolores remembered that such courses were offered several times during the year by Campus Ministry.

"Oh no. That wouldn't be practical, would it? Make arrangements in Minneapolis. They'll give you a certificate. I'll need that."

"How long does it take?" Dudley asked.

"Oh, it varies. Sometimes it is only a weekend. At other times . . ." His hand with fluttering fingers moved before his face. "The reason behind it is sound."

It was important that the couple knew the nature of the sacrament of matrimony, the indissolubility of marriage, the rights and wrongs of marital life.

"Above all, you must be of one mind about what you are doing."

At the Morris Inn, Dolores joined her mother in her room. Dudley looked into the bar where a man of enormous proportions was speaking to a young woman. There was a huge bottle of mineral water on the table before him. Dudley sat at the bar, was served, and still the fat man was on the same sentence. It exfoliated, ramified, returned upon itself, became ever more complicated, and then, at last, rose in finality, ending with a trochaic fall. Dudley applauded. The huge man laughed and the girl with him beamed with pleasure.

"Join us, join us."

Dudley was still with Prof. Roger Knight when Dolores came

down from her mother's room. She smiled at him and said, "You weren't here when I was a student, but I know who you are."

"You're a graduate of the university?"

"Don't ask the year."

When she told him her name it was clear, much to Dolores's surprise, that it was familiar to him and to the young woman. Soon it was clear why. The young woman was Nancy Beatty, Larry's intended, and she was a favorite of the professor. Nancy was obviously smart as a whip, but she seemed so young to Dolores, young and innocent. Mrs. Torre looked in, joined them, and immediately began an account of the labors of her day.

"We are stealing your reservation," Dolores said to Nancy.

"It's not really ours."

"Nor ours, really. Where will you get married?"

"We're thinking of Alumni Hall chapel."

"Is it large enough?"

"I don't think our wedding is going to be as grand as yours. My father is a professor."

"I take it you're not a graduate of this university," Roger Knight said to Dudley.

"Is that a requirement to drink here?"

Roger laughed. "I suppose the question sounded smug. I am not an alumnus either."

Nancy seemed shy and a little intimidated by Dolores, and this made her intent on winning the girl's confidence. She began to think of the girl as herself years ago when she and Larry were students. Dudley had told Roger Knight he was a graduate of the University of Chicago, and this had gotten the professor going on the golden years of that institution.

"Hutchins, Adler, the whole effort to recover liberal education.

An amazing, and I daresay unintended, consequence was the entrance into the Catholic Church of many students who came under their influence."

"Not much of that when I was there."

"You mean Bellow and Bloom, those fellows. But it has started up again, a group called *Lumen Christi*. Tom Levergood has visited me several times."

Bewildered, Dudley nodded.

"Of course there was Mark Van Doren at Columbia and his student Thomas Merton."

"I don't know those names."

"Merton became a Trappist."

Dolores rescued him. Dudley's Catholicism was a thin veneer over his secular soul. She wondered if he even realized that what he had been up to with Bianca was sinful.

15 ╌╌╌╌╌╌▶ LARRY MORTON DID NOT KID
himself that seeing Dolores as often as he did
was not a welcome bonus of his extended stay in Minneapolis. What
he increasingly found hard to believe was that Dolores found Dudley Fyte attractive. Maybe he would have been reconciled to her
claiming the June 17 reservation at Sacred Heart if he hadn't met
Dudley and found out what a jerk he was. Ten minutes with the condescending lawyer and Larry had been ready to take a swing at him.
And then Dolores had shown up at his hotel, and it seemed obvious
to Larry that she was far less committed to Fyte than claiming the
reservation they both had made years ago suggested.

"Larry, he really isn't like that."

"He gives a pretty good imitation then."

When Fyte himself appeared in the entrance of the bar off the
lobby of the Radisson, Larry had been sure that the fight that hadn't
happened was now on, but the guy disappeared. Maybe he should
have told Dolores then and there. What kind of a fiancé would come
spying on his girl and then not have the guts to come in and ask
what was going on? Larry felt he had won Round One.

But what prize was he fighting for? Dolores? If so, how was he
any better than Fyte? He tried to think of Nancy and feel guilty, but
suddenly he found it hard to form a clear image of the girl he was
going to marry. Being with Dolores had given the past priority over
the present. It was as if they had a first and unbroken claim on one
another, he and Dolores. But his moral unease diminished when he

told himself he was protecting Dolores. He couldn't just sit by and watch her marry a jerk like Dudley Fyte.

And then, in Mendota, Dolores told him about Dudley and the older woman.

"You've got to be kidding."

"He says it's all over with."

"And you believe him?"

"Of course I believe him."

"But what kind of guy carries on with a woman twice his age?"

"She's not *that* old, Larry."

For something that was supposedly over and done with, Bianca Primero played a large role in Dudley's life. When Larry began tailing Fyte, he justified it by saying he was looking out for Dolores. Maybe there were more Biancas in Dudley's life. It turned out that there was just the same one. He couldn't follow Fyte through the security check of the building he led Larry to, but Larry parked and went up to the structure that flanked one side of the entry.

"Hi, Norma."

"Who are you?"

He looked at his chest. "I forgot my name tag."

She looked down at hers. "So you passed the eye test."

"It's not upside down from this angle."

She grinned grudgingly. "Funny. What do you want?"

"That car that just drove in?"

"What about it?"

"You know the guy in it?"

"Who are you to ask?"

"You don't have to answer if you don't want to. Anyway, I know who he is. The question is, where is he going?"

It took awhile, but Norma liked him; he could feel it—either that or he was better than just sitting there bored. In the end, he primed the pump.

"Does the name Bianca Primero mean anything to you?"

She made a face and shook her head. "You know who that guy is and you know who he comes here to see, so why the questions?"

"To show you what a good detective I am."

"Are you a detective?"

"If I were, would I admit it?"

"Get outta here."

"You've been a great help."

Leave 'em laughing. Larry himself felt like laughing triumphantly. So goofing off with Bianca was a thing of the past, was it?

Anything but. Tailing Dudley Fyte became an avocation. Larry became convinced that if Dudley married Dolores, he would go on seeing Bianca afterward. He said as much, delicately, to Dolores, not that he told her he had been following Dudley around.

"That's more of less what she said when we had lunch."

Dolores's account of her lunch with the allegedly former mistress of the man she had agreed to marry should have been the end of the whole thing.

"She won't let him go," Larry said.

"He has a say about that."

"Let her have him."

Larry felt helpless. What could he tell Dolores about Dudley that she didn't essentially know already?

"Dolores, you can't marry him."

"You're a fine one to talk."

She took his remark to come from disappointed love. And her response suggested the same. They stared at one another, and suddenly she was in his arms and they were gripped by a madness, as if by multiplying kisses they could erase the lost years.

"What about Nancy?" Dolores asked, when calm returned.

"I don't know."

"Don't you? I've met her, you know. In The Morris Inn when we went down . . ." She stopped and tears filled her eyes. "Oh, Larry. What are we doing to them? What are we doing to ourselves?"

"We should never have broken up."

"I'm beginning to wonder if we ever did."

He was left confused by this turn of events, and so was she. When they were apart, Dolores would repent the renewal of their love. It wasn't right. They were both engaged to other people. Again and again, he had to win her back. But he feared that by some quirk she might drift away from him, out of reach entirely. So he kept on following Dudley Fyte. He followed him the night he broke into the house on Lake of the Isles.

16   ➤ PHILIP KNIGHT FLEW TO MIN-
neapolis with the list Whelan had prepared
of the stolen items that had arrived at the Notre Dame Archives.
Joseph Primero looked at it in silence, then passed it to Waldo Hermes.

"Check it out, will you, Waldo?"

Primero told Hermes to leave them and when they were alone
said to Phil, "I wonder if Waldo is behind all this."

"The package that was sent to Notre Dame was sent from your
wife's address."

"It was!"

"Of course, anyone could have put down her name and address
as sender."

"You say they were letters?"

"Of Cardinal Newman."

"I don't recall Waldo mentioning letters. But why would someone
do this?"

"What reason might your wife have?"

To ask the question was to have the unspoken answer vibrate in
the room. Primero nodded. "She could be playing a little vindictive
game with me."

"By stealing rare books?"

"Can you steal what you own?"

"You think she took these things?"

"Such things mean nothing to her. Even if she has some sense of their monetary value, she doesn't understand what they are."

Phil felt that he had done nothing Primero had hired him to do. The Newman letters had arrived safely at the Notre Dame Archives through no effort of his own. He was almost glad that not everything had been sent to Notre Dame. If Bianca Primero had the still-missing items, Phil intended to get them back. Joseph Primero might regard his wife as joint owner of his collection, but that is something they could quarrel about after the items were back where they belonged.

It was a short drive from Lake of the Isles to Highland Village but long enough for Phil to talk to Roger on his cell phone and review with him everything that had happened since they first came to Minneapolis to speak with Joseph Primero about the missing items in his collection. Picking up on Primero's own ill-concealed suspicion of Waldo Hermes at the time, Phil asked Roger about the possibility that it was an in-house crime.

"A man as knowledgeable as Hermes could certainly appropriate items in his care and divert suspicion."

"But he hasn't."

"I mean serious suspicion. Of course he is at the top of the list. He would know that."

"Right up there with the flown wife."

A long pause while the significance of the remark failed to get through to Roger.

"Roger, you saw Hermes." The curator was what Roger called hirsute, not exactly Lon Cheney as the wolf man but having far more than the average allotment of hair. His beard grew high on his cheekbones, his hairline was an inch above his brows, which formed thatched roofs over his spectacles. His eyes seemed to have just stopped rolling to form a losing combination. An unlit pipe through which he breathed as if from the bottom of some sea of self-absorption sent out puffs of stale air as he exhaled. But speaking of his metier transformed him. Fluent, even eloquent, he had clearly impressed Roger, and that was good enough for Phil. He found it perfectly plausible that so interesting a fellow might be attractive to Bianca Primero. "It must be a source of constant temptation for him," Roger mused.

"The wife?"

Roger was bewildered. "No, no. Working with such priceless materials, manuscripts, first editions, rare codices. How could their custodian fail to regard them as his own? The so-called owner and collector must come to seem an imposter."

"So he begins to make them his own?"

"Why should he? Everything is already his insofar as such treasures can belong to anyone. He is closer to them than Primero; it is his whole life."

"So you think Hermes is out."

"Not necessarily. It makes little sense if he is the thief, but then crime seldom makes sense."

That Bianca Primero resented her husband's absorption in his books and manuscripts was clear from his remarks and their earlier interview with her. The more she withdrew from him, the closer he became to his collection. Had she stolen items and then sent them to Notre Dame to get her husband's attention? It was a gesture that fitted in with what Phil had been told of her and with his own impression from his one brief encounter.

There was no answer to his ring, and Phil sought out the manager of the condominium. This turned out to be a thin young woman with a crew cut and a tilt to her jaw that seemed to dare him to say something.

"Bianca Primero doesn't answer her bell."

"So?" The woman's eyes were green. Phil wanted to comment on them, to move closer and study them. The jaw lifted another degree.

"Tinted contacts," she said. "The lenses are green."

"Nice."

This almost flustered her. "So she doesn't answer her bell. What do you want me to do?"

"Let me into her apartment."

"Ha!"

"You can be with me all the time." Phil showed her his license.

"This is a New York license." But there was respect rather than skepticism in her voice.

"I work for the husband."

"If you can call him that."

"They're estranged."

"You ever meet her?"

"Oh yes. A lot more than tinted contacts."

"She likes young guys."

Phil leaned back against her desk. He had a sense they would get along. "Look, Norm . . ."

"How did you know I'm called that?"

Phil pointed at her name tag: NORMA RIGLER.

"But you said Norm."

Phil shrugged. He could tell her he thought of her as a tomboy, but who knew what reaction that might get? Saying nothing proved wise. She picked up her keys and tossed them from hand to hand. She might have been picking petals off a daisy or flipping a coin.

"I haven't seen her for two days. That's unusual. Her car is in its stall. A Jag-u-ar. There's no one with her now."

Clearly Norma knew what was going on in her building.

"I was going to check on her anyway. You can come along."

They went up in the service elevator, and Norma let them in a back door that led into the laundry.

"Hello," Norma called. "Hello, hello. It's Norm."

Phil intended to search the apartment for the missing Newman materials but was unsure he would recognize them. But then, there was only one small shelf of books in the living room. Norma had gone into the kitchen and from there to the living room. Phil took the hallway and went back to the master bedroom.

She might have been asleep, lying on the large circular bed as if arranged there for maximum effect. A sheet covered her casually. Venus rising from the waters. Her hair was splayed out on the silken pillow. Pills spilled from several open bottles lying on the spread. It was the open, staring eyes that told Phil she was dead.

"My God!" Norma was beside him and tried to push past him into the room. He stopped her.

"Better not. We don't want to disturb anything."

"Is she dead?"

Phil nodded.

"Don't you want to check and make sure?"

No need to comment on the odor that competed with the various artificial scents that clung to the room.

"She's dead all right."

They might have been observing a moment of silence.

"Better call the police," Phil advised.

"She was old, you know, but she took care of herself."

"Maybe it wasn't a natural death, Norm."

Silk fabric drifted scarflike from her throat and lay like her hair upon the pillow. The murder weapon? The pressure eased once she was dead? Her posture could not have been that in which she had died. Phil guessed that someone had taken the care to arrange her almost lovingly on the bed.

Norma called 911 and then Phil called homicide and talked to a Lieutenant Swenson.

"Don't touch anything."

"Lieutenant, I'm a PI." He hesitated. "New York license."

Norma wanted to be downstairs when the 911 crew arrived to hold down the disturbance. Left alone, Phil searched the apartment for the first edition of the *Apologia*. He started looking in the bedroom but it wasn't there. It wasn't on the shelf in the living room, among the travel books. And then there was the sound of the back door opening and Norma appeared, followed by two uniformed cops and a blasé teams of paramedics.

Lieutenant Swenson came within the half hour. Tall, vacant blue eyes, mandatory blond hair.

"What's a New York PI doing here?" he asked, after a quick inspection of the bedroom.

"I was hired by her husband."

"He worried about her?"

"In a sense."

"That would be Joseph Primero?"

"You know him?"

"I know who he is."

"I'd like to be the one who tells him about this."

"Where you going to find him?"

"At his house on Lake of the Isles."

"Minneapolis." Swenson was a Saint Paul cop. "I'll come by there later."

And so Philip Knight went off to tell Joseph Primero that his wife, Bianca, was dead.

PART TWO

17

THE NEXT TWENTY-FOUR HOURS were hectic, and Phil wished that Roger was with him.

"I could fly up there, Phil."

"Alone?"

"I'd have to go first class. Or buy two coach tickets."

"Let's just keep in touch for now, Roger."

There was the telephone, of course, but more importantly, E-mail. Phil had finally subjected himself to Roger's instructions on the subject, a blur of unintelligibility.

"Don't ever try to teach someone how to drive a car, Roger."

"I don't know how to drive."

"Let's go over it again."

They went over it until Phil had it—the skill, and a remarkable little portable computer on which to exercise it. He got on the web via his cell phone and this made for an almost instantaneous method of communication. Thus it was that Phil followed up his phone conversation with Roger with a lengthy E-mail message.

Dear Roger

Bianca Primero was found dead in her apartment, apparently a suicide, though the body seemed arranged on the bed after she had died with a scarf, suggestive of strangulation, around her neck. Perhaps this was a deliberate effort to negate the fact that she was dead. A loving effort.

Joseph received the news in eerie silence. He was in conference with Waldo Hermes when I got there but sent Waldo away. Joseph thought I had come simply to report on my visit to his wife. When I told him she was dead, he sat in complete silence for several minutes, like a statue. But then tears were running down his cheeks, and his chest shook with suppressed sobs. His expression never really changed. When he did speak, it was to ask if it had been a break-in. That's when I told him about the bottles of pills and how the body was arranged. He swore. I think it was the first profanity I ever heard from him. More later. Phil.

Phil wrote this message on the sunporch, and when he turned from his laptop Waldo Hermes was standing behind him.

"Bianca Primero is dead."

The curator nodded. "I was eavesdropping."

"You don't seem surprised."

"This isn't the best time to say it, but I'm glad she is dead. Glad for him. A man with his interests and the wealth and intelligence to pursue them being jerked around by that aging femme fatale is not a pretty sight. Why couldn't he just accept that she was gone and concentrate on what he truly liked."

"She was his wife, Waldo. I'm sure he loved her more than his books."

"You've met her. You've seen what a shallow, vacuous tramp she is."

Phil smiled. "Reason is not the sole guide in these matters. And they had been through a lot together."

"The lost son?" The curator made what must have been a face behind the mask of hair.

"It defined his life, Waldo."

This conviction had come slowly to Phil. Father Carmody had suggested that neither Bianca nor Joseph had ever gotten over the loss of their only child. The boy had died while Joseph was serving with the navy; and whether or not he blamed Bianca for the loss, she seemed to think he did. Of course she had complained about Joseph's collection of books, but that scarcely accounted for the bitterness she felt toward him. While Phil was telling Primero about the death of his wife, he found himself looking at the framed color photograph of a little boy, standing in sunlight, a bed of hollihocks behind him, prominent on the table behind Primero's chair. Doubtless this was the lost son. When Joseph fell silent, he too turned to the photograph.

"But did it define hers?" Waldo asked.

"You don't think so?"

"I don't think she thought of anything but her own momentary amusement—ever."

Phil let that go uncommented on.

Waldo said, "What do you know of Dudley Fytc?"

"What should I know?"

"He's Bianca's gigolo."

"Is that how it was?"

"He was half Bianca's age. She had the money."

"What does he do?"

"He is a lawyer."

"Successful?"

"He will never be in the same class as Joseph Primero."

Waldo seemed to think that loyalty to his employer entailed despising Primero's estranged wife. How ironic that Joseph Primero had half suggested that Waldo might be responsible for the items missing from the collection.

Detective Swenson arrived then, and they all gathered in the kitchen where Waldo made coffee.

"You've already heard the tragic news?" Swenson said to Primero.

"Philip Knight told me."

"Yes. He found the body, in the company of the manager of the condominium." Swenson took a cigarette from a package, rolled it in his fingers, and began to stuff it back in the package.

"You can smoke if you want," Primero said.

"I've quit." He shoved the package back into his pocket. He asked Phil, "Why *were* you at the apartment?"

"I wanted to talk with her as part of an assignment I'm on."

"I asked him to talk with Bianca." Primero rose. "Look. I'm in no mood to talk now. I am perfectly willing to speak with you later, but for now . . ." He took a deep breath. "Where have they taken her body?"

"Downtown. There has to be an autopsy."

"Don't I have to okay that?"

"Aren't you divorced?"

"Certainly not."

"Do you object to an autopsy?"

"I object to nothing that helps discover whoever killed my wife."

Between them, Phil and Waldo told Swenson what they knew. It was easier to speak of the Primeros without Joseph there, off on the terrible errand of seeing his wife laid out in the city morgue, wanting to see her before the autopsy began.

"They were estranged, not divorced?"

"Married in name only," Waldo Hermes added.

"You work right here in the house?" Swenson asked the curator.

"Yes. I live here too since she left. Over the garage in what were

110

once servants' quarters." His beard rearranged itself. A sardonic smile?

"How long ago did she move out?"

Waldo actually looked at his watch. "Four, five years."

"Big fight?"

"Fight! He was like Chamberlain at Munich."

"Explain that."

"She wrapped him around her little finger. She did unforgivable things and he was the one who felt guilty. She was punishing him for something, maybe for not being an idiot like herself."

Unobtrusively, Phil looked up Fyte, Dudley, in the telephone directory. A residence number and another for his office. In the kitchen, he dialed the latter and a voice said, "Kunert and Skye."

"What is your address?"

"I beg your pardon."

"Where is Kunert and Skye located?"

The receptionist rattled off a downtown Minneapolis address.

After he parked and started up the street to the building in which Kunert and Skye were located, Phil heard someone call his name. He turned and there was Larry Morton.

18

NANCY BEATTY, IN THE FINAL semester of her senior year, was taking a directed reading course with Roger Knight on the novels of Barbey d'Aureville. They met in the Knight apartment to save him the trouble of going to his campus office. That is why Nancy was there when Phil called to say that he had run into Larry Morton in Minneapolis.

"Is he still there," Roger said.

"His new firm asked him to stay a few days. It gives him a chance to check with realtors about housing." Nancy hesitated. "And he thinks we might still have our wedding at Sacred Heart Basilica."

"I thought that was settled."

"It's a long story."

Nancy tried to put the best possible face on the story that her fiancé had been engaged before and had arranged to be married in the campus church.

"How long ago was that?"

"Years ago. Six years ago at least."

"And the Basilica didn't hold the reservation?"

"Oh, that was never the problem. Now there seems to be some difficulty with the other wedding."

"She is conceding the reservation?"

"She has no more claim to the reservation than Larry."

"And vice versa."

"I suppose."

"So what's the resolution?"

"Larry thinks she may call off her wedding."

An e-mail from Phil and then a call from Larry suggested why such a resolution might be at hand.

Dear Roger

Told you I saw Larry Morton when I was on my way to call on Dudley Fyte. When I told Larry where I was going, he stopped dead in his tracks and stared at me. Turns out he knows Dudley. Or has met him. And hates his guts. The darndest thing. You know that Larry got engaged as an undergraduate and he and the girl made an appointment at the Basilica for years later and then drifted apart and forgot about the reservation. The other girl claimed it, intending to marry Dudley Fyte. I think Larry was angrier with Dudley than with the girl— her name is Dolores Torre. I didn't tell him that Dudley had been mixed up with Bianca Primero. My point in talking with Dudley was to figure out whether I should tell Swenson about him. Now that he is engaged to marry Nancy, it would almost be a favor to Larry to turn suspicion on Dudley so he can claim the reservation. That may happen anyway. The police will learn of Dudley from the young woman who manages the condominium in which Bianca lived. Or from Primero himself. After our little talk I felt like throwing Dudley to the wolves as a personal favor to myself. He came out into the reception area to talk to me, no offer to sit down, just stood there, feet apart, arms folded, and told me to make it quick, he was a busy man. So I told him I had news about Bianca Primero. Before I could go on, he demanded to know who I was and I told him and then he just turned on his heel and went into his office and closed the door. I followed him and knocked on the door, then opened it. Fortunately he hadn't locked it. I said, "You didn't give me a chance to tell you about Bianca Primero." He told me to get the hell out of his office. He picked up the phone and asked for security. I said: "She's dead, Mr Fyte. She was found dead in her apartment, strangled." He asked why I was telling him this. I turned to leave. Parting shot: "Think of it as a little warning before the police get here."

Larry Morton was waiting for me when I left Dudley, wanted to know what it was all about so I told him. I think he is worried about the girl Dudley is engaged to marry.

Larry's call to Nancy was made to the Knight apartment when he did not find her at home. He had talked with Phil about the death of Bianca Primero.

"The man Dolores is supposed to marry was apparently mixed up with her," Larry said.

"Mixed up?"

"I don't know the details."

Nancy found it easy to share Larry's concern about Dolores, having met her in the Morris Inn. It was one thing to know that there had been someone else long ago, but now the woman became more real and Nancy imagined how awful it must be to learn that the man you were going to marry was, well, mixed up with an older married woman.

"I can't believe she would fall for such a nerd," Larry said.

"Be careful. She may want you back."

"Ha."

After Nancy had hung up, Roger found her pensive and not in a mood to talk about *Le prêtre marié* of d'Aureville so he chattered on about the conservative Catholics who had deplored the French Revolution—De Maistre, Bonald. But after a time he realized he was talking to himself.

"When is Larry coming back?"

"He didn't say."

114

"Has he found a place?"

Bad question. Apparently that had not come up. Of course Larry would be working in Minneapolis and would be kept busy by people at the firm that had hired him.

They did not go the full hour and little of that had been spent on the topic at hand. Roger watched Nancy go out to her car and felt foreboding. She drove off and he shuffled back to his computer, hoping for another message from Phil, not a realistic expectation. Nancy had not known Bianca Primero so the woman's death did not fully register with her. There was no message from Phil but there was one from Greg Whelan.

19

WENDY, THE HEAD ARCHIVIST, was excited about the arrival of the materials from the Primero Collection that Greg Whelan had placed carefully on her desk. The arrangement had been an unusual one, Primero's collection entered by Greg into the Archives database but not yet in possession. The university had offered to underwrite the purchase of additional items, but Primero had refused. He would add to his promised gift himself.

"We may have to send that stuff back," Greg said.

The head archivist frowned at the suggestion. "I was thinking of a display in the library concourse. A foretaste of the treasures coming our way."

"But these things were stolen from his collection. He didn't send them."

"Then who did?"

"Apparently the one who stole them."

"That doesn't make sense."

"I know."

It made more sense when he and Roger Knight talked about it over great bowls of spaghetti prepared by the massive Huneker Chair of Catholic Studies. Greg had received a warmer than usual welcome when he showed up at the Knight apartment. Roger obviously missed his brother.

"How long will he stay in Minneapolis?"

"There's been a murder, Greg. Mrs. Primero."

"Good Lord! There goes one suspect."

"How do you mean?"

"She couldn't have stolen the things that were sent here."

"Why not?"

"The return address on the FedEx box? Just Primero, but an address in Saint Paul. Not *his* address."

"That doesn't mean she didn't steal what she sent."

"Do you think she did?"

"I don't think she didn't."

Roger poured another glass of Chianti for Greg and more ice water for himself. The professor's account of the troubled Primero marriage invited gratitude for the single state he and Roger had been wise enough to choose—if it had been a choice. Marital strife was apparently more widespread than one would have thought, however mysterious that must seem to two bachelors. The story became more complicated when Roger went on to speak of Mrs. Primero's affair with a younger man.

"The man who is to marry Larry Morton's fiancée."

"Nancy Beatty?"

"No, no. This is another girl, someone he went with as an undergraduate. They thought they were in love; they planned to marry. They actually made a reservation at Sacred Heart. It was when Larry went to the Basilica to claim the reservation that he found his old girlfriend already had claimed it in order to marry this fellow Dudley Fyte."

"Who was having an affair with Mrs. Primero."

"It is an odd situation."

"And now it is hooked up with Notre Dame."

Roger didn't contest this, of course, but Whelan felt called upon to qualify his remark. "Quite accidentally, of course."

"Yes," Roger said, and his mind seemed to drift off.

Later, still feeling the glow of the Chianti, Greg sat up late and tried to sort out all of the strange information Roger had passed on to him. Two Notre Dame undergraduates precipitously make a reservation to marry some years after they graduate, but they drift apart, find other mates, and then both want to make use of the reservation arranged so long ago but with another spouse in mind. Larry had flown off to Minneapolis to straighten it out with the other girl, Dolores Torre. And Minneapolis is where the Knight brothers had gone to investigate a theft from a priceless collection that was destined for Notre Dame. While they were gone, some of the stolen items arrived at the Notre Dame Archives. Apparently the theft had been meant to make a statement rather than to take possession of the stolen items. If Mrs. Primero had taken the things, for whatever reason, and had sent only some letters—but such letters—to the Archives, other missing things should be in her home.

No one knew better than Greg Whelan what the value of the complete Primero Collection was. The stolen items were invaluable, there was little doubt of that, but they formed a small part of a vast number of things that Joseph Primero had purchased over the years. The wealthy businessman had a singular eye for rare books, and the portion of his collection devoted to nineteenth-century Catholicism, while large, was but a fraction of the whole. Greg Whelan could not help envying Waldo Hermes who spent his days with the Primero Collection.

Like other archivists and curators, Greg Whelan had developed a proprietary attitude toward the things entrusted to him. He was but an associate director—he had no ambition for promotion even if his speech impediment had not stood in his way—but that was rank enough to feel a kind of ownership toward the marvels in the Notre Dame Archives. He already salivated in anticipation of the arrival of the Primero Collection at Notre Dame. Imagine what it must be

118

for Hermes to have it presently at his fingertips. And imagine how he must feel about the theft of things that had been placed in his care.

He felt suddenly virtuous for having finally turned over the New-man letters to Wendy. He had of course made photocopies for him-self.

20 ----▸ TO SAY THAT DUDLEY FYTE was ready when the police came to talk to him about the death of Bianca Primero would have been an understatement. His reaction to the private detective showing up at the office had been all wrong. And it had drawn unnecessary attention to the visit. Amy had avoided his eyes, banging away on her computer keyboard, pretending not to have noticed. Since then he had been rehearsing what he would say when the police asked him about Bianca.

"She was a dear friend."

But they would know she had been more than that by the time they called on him.

"I loved her like an aunt."

"She undertook to tutor me in the arts."

It was difficult to say any of these with a straight face. How could he rehearse without knowing what the questions would be? But finally Detective Swenson came and all the rehearsing seemed idiotic.

"I want your help in investigating the death of Bianca Primero, Mr. Fyte. There are a few odds and ends that have to be cleared up."

"Of course I'll help."

"I guess you knew her as well as anyone."

"I knew her very well."

"I'm glad you're not going to beat around the bush. Norma, the superintendent of the building in which the death occurred, gives a very vivid description of you."

Norma? That would be the boyish young woman who thought she could watch others through her fingers and not be noticed. She had been a little joke between Bianca and Dudley. "If she keeps a diary, we're in it."

Remembering Bianca's remark now, Dudley thought that Norma would not need a diary to recall things harmful to him.

"Bianca and I had been intimate. I guess there's no point in denying that. She was older than I. That was part of the attraction. But it had ended amicably. I am now engaged to be married."

"Mrs. Primero knew that?"

"It was the reason for the alteration in our relations. I told her of course."

"What was her reaction?"

"She took it very well. Almost too well. Not very flattering. She took my fiancée to lunch and made us the gift of a very valuable painting."

"She didn't seem suicidal?"

Dudley gave it some thought. "She had a very volatile temperament, ups and downs. I don't know. Maybe."

"How did you first learn of her death?"

"One of your colleagues. Knight?"

"He's a private detective, hired by Mr. Primero."

"He made a bit of a scene at my office."

"The reason I said suicidal, I wondered if she was depressed after you dropped her. Anyway, there was no note."

Dudley leaned back in his chair. Swenson looked at him, as if expecting a response, then said, "Do you know what drugs she took?"

"Drugs!"

"Sedatives, uppers, downers, Prozac?"

"I believe she sometimes took sleeping pills."

"While you were there?"

Dudley took umbrage at this. Swenson was too damned interested in his relationship with Bianca. "That's not a damned bit funny." He shook his head. "I can't believe she's dead."

"There were several bottles of sleeping pills at the scene."

Dudley thought of people going through Bianca's apartment, opening drawers, snooping around.

"Mr. Fyte, I want you to give the matter some thought. Anything you might remember that would help this investigation I want to know. If something occurs to you, call this number."

He handed Dudley his card. The two men rose. After he had let Swenson out, Dudley closed the door carefully. He walked slowly back to his living room and sat once more where he had been sitting when Swenson mentioned suicide. Was this how a condemned man feels when the reprieve from the governor comes through?

But Dudley's thoughts had gone on to how he might now speak of all this with Dolores.

21 — → WHEN ROGER TOLD HIM OF the return address on the package in which the Newman letters had come to the Notre Dame Archives, Phil checked out the package mailers in the vicinity of Bianca Primero's apartment. Roger had faxed him a photocopy of the FedEx receipt that had come with the box. The nearest package mailer was on Highland Parkway, in the shadow of the water tower, at least late in the afternoon, and Phil had to wait in line. Others were lined up behind him when he got to the counter. He showed the harried young woman the photocopy. She just stared at him.

"Was this sent from here?"

"A piece of paper?" She let her mouth hang open.

"This is a copy of the form attached to a FedEx package . . ."

"Can I help you?"

It was the manager, a thin man with bulging eyes and a neck that emerged from the too large collar of his starched white shirt as from a noose before the trapdoor is opened. He was more anxious to stop Phil from blocking traffic to the counter than to help him.

"Do you keep records of packages sent from here?"

The manager's glasses were perched on top of his head. He peered at the photocopy. "Who's asking?"

"I'm a private investigator." Phil opened his wallet. The manager leaned forward and his glasses slid off his head and onto his nose, which he wrinkled to keep them from sliding farther.

"I've never seen one of those before." He pushed his glasses back atop his head. "We have carbons of all transactions."

He sat behind a desk, both hands dropped and simultaneously two drawers were pulled open. He looked at Phil. "That saves the back. Yank with just one hand and . . ." He twisted in his chair. "What was the date?"

The carbon Phil was shown didn't help. On it, too, PRIMERO was printed. "I don't suppose anyone would remember a transaction on that date."

One side of the manager's mouth went up, his lips parted. The smile was more like a snarl. "Do you know how many transactions have taken place at that counter since you came in?"

"Good point."

Going out to his car, he recalled a cardinal rule of his trade. Even disappointment is a kind of discovery. He had hoped to see Bianca Primero's handwriting, thus confirming that she had indeed sent the Newman letters to Notre Dame. Her printed name neither proved nor disproved that, whereas her handwriting would have settled it.

The officer at Bianca Primero's apartment was less welcoming than Norma at the gatehouse.

"Can't let you in. The place is not secure yet."

"Would you mind checking with Swenson?"

"Checking what?"

"Tell him Det. Philip Knight requests admission to see Bianca Primero's apartment."

The officer's expression changed. "You from Minneapolis?"

"I don't blame you for being careful about detectives from strange cities."

The officer stepped aside. "Go on in."

Phil didn't move. "I'd feel better if you checked with Swenson."

They went into the apartment together so the cop could use the phone. "I'm going to use the bathroom," Phil said.

It was when he passed the room in which the body of Bianca was found that his angle of vision picked out the pink wastebasket beside her vanity table. Phil picked it up and took it into the bathroom. Among the Kleenex was a wad of paper that was not tissue. One glance at it after he unfolded it caused Phil to stuff it in his shirt pocket. He left the wastebasket in the bathroom. He flushed the toilet and headed for the kitchen. The cop met him halfway.

"He said, 'Hell no!' "

"I thought he might. Well, it was worth a try."

"He said you were a private investigator." Curiosity, contempt, simple wonder? It was hard to say.

"I flunked out of public school."

He stopped and talked with Norma on the way to his car. "Still knocking 'em dead."

"Be careful, you may be next."

In his car he was about to examine the slip of paper, but caution gripped him. He drove off, stopped at a bar, ordered a beer, and then, in the dim light, got out the slip of paper he had found in Bianca's wastebasket. It was a list: a list of Newman items. Phil put the slip carefully in his wallet then sipped his beer in a meditative mood. The certainty he had hoped to gain from the visit to the package mailer was provided by this slip of paper. The items on it were written in Bianca's hand, he was sure of it. And the items were those missing from the Primero Collection. So much for facts. He would hold off trying to find a meaning in them until he talked to Roger. He glanced at his watch. Give it an hour.

"Read them again, will you, Phil?"

Phil did, pronouncing carefully. Roger repeated them as if there was an echo on the line.

THE PRESENT HAD SIGNIFI-cance for Waldo Hermes insofar as it affected the past that was his passion—or at least the artifacts and achievements of the past. The constant ongoing flux was difficult to assess, but once frozen in the past it had a permanent value. He had never liked Bianca and vice versa. It was his arrival in the house on Lake of the Isles that had eventually provided her with an excuse to leave. She professed to find him physically loathsome, a disturbing presence in the house. Such claims baffled Waldo, but doubtless they were simply the rationalizations of a fed-up wife.

"She hates my books," Primero had told him.

"That's impossible."

Primero smiled indulgently. Of course he understood Waldo's reaction, but women are different from men. Waldo required no instruction on that score; from adolescence, females had frightened and unnerved him.

"I'll keep out of her way."

"Just do your job."

Waldo's admiration for Primero was of course based primarily on the collection. As he became more and more familiar with the treasures Primero had amassed, he could only salute the man who had had the taste, as well as the money, to bring these things together. Primero's enormous wealth meant little to him: He was proud of what he had accomplished and he appreciated the items he bought for his collection, but he did not think of himself as the owner.

"You are the curator and custodian, Waldo, but that is all I am too. Collecting is a rescuing operation, in large part just making sure that things are not lost. But once they have been gathered, they cannot really be possessed by any one person. Hence, the art galleries of the world. The private collector is a way station on the road to public ownership."

"Then I will enjoy the way station."

Primero's altruism seemed sincere enough. Despite his small stature he became a moral giant to Waldo. But the curator never understood Primero's continued love for his wife despite her flamboyant infidelities. When he ventured to say something about this, Primero's reaction surprised him.

"It has been said that to understand everything is to forgive everything. Not true, of course. But the inability to forgive is worse when it concerns oneself. Bianca was a mother once, Waldo. That is the key."

But there were no children. Waldo did not understand.

"Not any longer."

So it was that he learned of the dead child and knew the significance of the photograph on the table behind Primero's desk chair. Shared grief draws people together. Sometimes. The Primeros were the exception, the couple that is driven asunder by a loss that could have sealed their love forever. The lost child made Joseph a more sympathetic figure, but for Bianca Waldo felt almost contempt. What did she gain from making a fool of herself and shredding her husband's heart at the same time?

Waldo took refuge in the past. In his work he was able to forget the troubles of his employer. And after Bianca left the house and took an apartment, something like peace seemed to descend upon the house on Lake of the Isles. Several weeks ago Waldo began to get glimpses of a familiar-looking Jaguar. He'd tried to dismiss his anxiety. Jaguars are not rare animals in the Lake of the Isles area. But he was on the *qui vive* for its return, if it was indeed Bianca cruising past the home she had left. It was Bianca. Once she was alone at the wheel, another time she was in the passenger seat with a young man at the wheel. On another occasion, which he was about to dismiss as a false alarm, he amended the judgment. The young man behind the wheel and alone in the car was the one who had driven by with Bianca. A week later the robbery occurred.

What to do? There was no need to say anything in order to cause Joseph Primero to suspect his wife of the theft. Of course Primero suspected Bianca, but he didn't want to. He both embraced and rejected the idea.

"She could have," Primero said, in an agony of loss. "She might have. But I simply cannot imagine her walking into this house and taking those items."

"Did she keep her key?"

Primero looked as if the question surprised him. "This is her house. She is welcome to return here whenever she wants."

What a doormat the man was. It must be a disease, and do not tell me it is love, Waldo cautioned himself. Do not quote Shakespeare: "Love is not love which alters when it alteration finds," a sentiment seldom verified. A man might take much abuse from a woman if it functioned as a kind of foreplay, but the Primeros had long since stopped being spouses to one another. It was not her favors that gave Bianca the weapon she wielded against her docile husband. No, it was the child again. Bianca was not the wife of Joseph so much as the mother of the sainted child. She had a permanent and indissoluble hold on Joseph Primero.

No wonder Waldo felt that he himself had come under suspicion.

Joseph wanted to review again and again the circumstances of the theft, inspect again the places occupied by the missing items, ask one more time when Waldo had last seen them, touched them,

"We cannot assume that the discovery of the theft coincides with the time the theft occurred. How long might they have been missing?"

This question went to the heart of Waldo's reliability. As if anything in the collection could be missing for a day without his noticing it. He had acquired an intuitive sense of the presence of his charges. That is how he had verified the theft. An odd pang as he passed an alcove, a quick glance, and he had known the *Apologia* was missing. An inference swifter than logic led him to the cabinet where the pamphlet version of the work was kept. Its absence turned him to the Newman letters. Nothing was missing there. Thus, in a glance, he had become aware both of the fact and the extent of the theft.

Joseph's unwillingness to report the theft to the police led to the hiring of Philip Knight, the main advantage of which, so far as Waldo was concerned, was that it enabled him to renew face-to-face acquaintance with Roger, the man who referred to himself as Notre Dame's permanent Goodyear Blimp. He had heard much of Roger from Greg Whelan.

"There was no forced entry?"

"No."

Roger hummed as he looked around Waldo's domain. "So the thief had a key?"

"Yes."

"Who might it be?"

"It might be me, of course. Or Mr. Primero."

"Or Mrs. Primero."

Waldo nodded. "Or Mrs. Primero."

It was because his wife was the obvious suspect that Primero ensured the failure of the Knight investigation. Only with the greatest reluctance did he okay their visit to Bianca.

"You mustn't make her think that I suspect her of anything."

When the brothers returned, it seemed clear to Waldo that Bianca was their candidate. It was equally clear that Joseph Primero would never accept this—or the consequences of accepting it. But the point did not depend upon Primero's acceptance. Waldo carefully selected some Newman letters and FedExed them to the Notre Dame Archives. The return address was Primero, the address was Bianca's in Highland Village. He sent the package off from a place near her apartment.

He knew that Bianca, through her protégé Dudley Fyte, had robbed the Primero Collection. The FedEx to the Notre Dame Archives should lead to the recovery of the stolen items from Bianca. But they had not yet been recovered when Bianca Primero was found dead in her apartment.

23 → NORMA SMOKED CIGARILLOS and inhaled the smoke so deeply it should have affected her feet. Exhaled, it made a thin cloud, but thick enough for Norma to look enigmatically through it at Philip Knight.

"How do you become a private detective?"

"You have to flunk a test."

"You need a license, don't you?"

"Norm, it is not as glamorous as it seems."

"What is? Friends of mine envy me this job, just loll around all day and not pay any rent for the privilege. I don't see those friends much anymore. Try to get away from this place. It's like baby-sitting a building."

"So what do you do all day?"

"Try to stay awake."

They were in Norma's office, one wall of which was filled with the monitors that brought in images from various points around the condominium complex.

"What do you do if something happens, call the police?"

There was a revolver on the desk, but it was difficult imagining the 110-pound tomboy being very effective with it.

"I can handle myself. Karate? I can split a block of wood with one movement of my hand." She narrowed her eyes. "Provided I have a hatchet in it, that is. Bianca is the first trouble there's been since I got here."

"Are you complaining?"

"Not even a murder in the building helps much."

"You mentioned young friends."

"Oh, you mean Mrs. Primero's young friends. Plural is pushing it. I only saw the one guy. My predecessor made it sound as if there would be a steady stream going up to her place."

"Is this the man?"

Phil took out the picture of Dudley Fyte and showed it to her.

"That's him. You think he's the murderer?"

"When did you last see him around?"

"If you're really serious, you could look at the tapes."

"Tapes?"

She nodded at the monitors. "Everything they see is taped. And kept here for a month."

"Let's see what you have for the week before Bianca's death?"

The tapes could have won an award for avant garde film. By and large, nothing happened. Andy Warhol's brick wall was as exciting. From time to time a car came or went. Norma had nicknames for the drivers, depending on the way they greeted her when they went past her post: Fix-o-dent, the Big Bad Wolf, Betty Boop.

"What did you call Bianca?"

"I didn't call them these names out loud."

"What name did you give Bianca?"

"The Mummy's Smile."

There was a sequence of Dudley talking with Norma. He was Mr. Personality. "If only I were older and richer," she said, but without much interest in her voice.

"When was that?"

"Two days before."

More inactivity. Even fast-forwarded, the security system seemed a massive waste of tape.

"We reuse it."

"How do you tape over nothing with nothing?"

"Get a load of this guy," Norma said, and there was the hairy face of Waldo Hermes peering up at Norma from his car. "Imagine reading his lips."

"Imagine his lips. Turn it up."

"She's expecting me," Hermes was saying.

"She left no word with me."

"Can you call her?"

Norma handed him a cell phone, and Hermes went out of sight in his car.

"Can you get more volume?" Phil asked.

"You wouldn't be able to hear him. I tried at the time."

"Did he get in?"

But even as he asked, Waldo was handing Norma the cell phone. Then he backed out of view.

"When was that?"

"It's on the tape, there at the bottom."

The date was the day Bianca was found dead.

Roger phoned with the puzzling news that the Newman letters that had arrived at the Notre Dame Archives were not on the list Phil had found in Bianca's wastebasket.

"What do you make of it?"

"The list itself is the first problem. Why would a woman who was going to take things from her husband's collection make a list of them?"

"You go first."

"One possibility is that someone dictated the list, and she wrote it down. Who could have given her such specific information?"

"Waldo?"

"Or Joseph Primero."

"Neither of them makes any sense, Roger. Why would Primero give his wife a list of things to steal from his collection? Why would Waldo? Roger, he hated Bianca's guts."

"The question is, are the other missing items in her apartment? What you found out about the FedEx package suggests someone was trying to bring Bianca under suspicion for the thefts from the Primero Collection."

"A frame-up."

"To cover the tracks of the real thief."

Even over five hundred miles, the two brothers communicated more than they said. Phil said, "I'll go see Waldo."

"Keep me posted."

24 THE EVENTUAL SYSTEMATIC search of Bianca's apartment by the police turned up nothing helpful. That the items missing from her husband's collection were not found in the apartment struck different people in different ways. Joseph Primero, affecting to think that it was absurd to imagine Bianca could have done such a thing, nonetheless looked relieved. Waldo Hermes looked incredulous when Phil passed the information on to him.

"Nothing? But that's impossible. I know she was behind the thefts."

"Know as in are certain?"

Waldo told Phil about the cruising Jaguar and the man who had sometimes accompanied Bianca in her drive-bys, and sometimes had gone by alone in the car.

"Have you told Swenson?"

"I didn't think I'd have to. Once suspicion turned to her. . . ."

"Because of the Newman letters you sent to Notre Dame?"

Waldo looked at Phil. "How do you know that?"

"It's true, isn't it?"

"That was meant to lead to a search of Bianca's apartment."

"They found nothing, Waldo."

"I can't believe it."

Waldo did not seem to realize that he had indicated where the missing items would be found. Bianca had an accomplice. The accomplice was almost certainly Dudley Fyte. If the missing items were not in Bianca's apartment, Fyte must still have them.

Phil had been hired to find the things stolen from Joseph Primero's collection, not to find whoever had killed his wife. He seemed to be doing both. But the investigation of Bianca's death was in the presumably able hands of the police.

"Two birds with one stone?" Roger said over the telephone from South Bend. "I'm not so sure."

"I told you what Waldo said."

"Oh, I believe that. Bianca sent Dudley for those things on the list you found, and he entered the house and took them,"

"Waldo tried to bring about a search of her apartment."

"By sending those letters here."

"Doesn't that surprise you?"

"Phil, Greg found some packages in which Waldo had sent things to the Archives before. The printing on those was like the putative one from Bianca."

"Why didn't you tell me?"

"I didn't have to, did I?"

"Roger, I still have not done what we were hired to do."

"Have you told Joseph Primero everything?"

Roger had been fascinated by the news that entries and exits to the condo in which Bianca had her apartment were taped. He called it a parody of omniscience. Why do we think what we do not see is more interesting than what we do? Surveillance cameras were a tribute to Bishop Berkeley.

"Roger, I haven't the faintest idea what you're talking about."

"*Esse est percipi.*"

"No kidding." And he loved the nicknames Norma devised. Phil told him all those he remembered, including Captain Midnight.

"Captain Midnight!"

Captain Midnight, the resident so called by Norma, always wore a crushed captain's cap and huge dark glasses, a pencil thin mustache, and a winning smile, flashed briefly as the tinted glass slid down and then quickly slid up again.

"I figure he's wearing a leather flying jacket," Norma said, "and a white silk scarf."

"What's his name?"

"Queedam. He has the penthouse."

When Philip talked to Joseph Primero and mentioned the likelihood that his wife had removed the missing items from the collection in the house on Lake of the Isles, Primero shook his head. "She didn't do it."

"You sound as if you know who did."

Primero looked at Phil with an agonized expression. "I don't want to get him in trouble."

"Him?"

"Waldo." Primero actually whispered the name.

Phil took him out onto the sunporch, where dozens of plants and flowers flourished. Then Primero told him of seeing the *Apologia* in Waldo's room. "It is an ironclad rule that nothing is to be taken from the library. Nothing. By anybody."

Phil found it hard to share Primero's sense of the seriousness of Waldo's offense.

"When he reported the theft, I was dumbstruck. The fact is I didn't believe it had happened . . ."

"You thought he might report items missing when they weren't?"

"Oh, they would be missing."

"But taken by Waldo?"

"I felt like a sneak going into his room. I told myself that he was just absentminded, that he had forgotten he had taken things to his room. That was when I saw the *Apologia.*"

"Hidden."

"If being put into a bookcase is being hidden."

"What about the other things?"

"That is the puzzle. The *Apologia* is gone. Waldo tells me he returned it to its place in the library—"

Roger reminded him by E-mail that Waldo was the single source of the claim that Bianca and her boyfriend had been casing the joint. Roger loved to lapse into such clichés, and they were obviously italicized when he spoke them; but he did not know how to create italics in E-mail messages.

"Good point," Phil replied.

Mulling it over and thinking of what Primero had told him led eventually to the following message.

Dear Roger.

Try this. Waldo steals everything that's missing and, to throw suspicion on Bianca, ships off a few letters to Notre Dame as if from her. The assumption will be that she and Dudley Fyte stole the other things, and even if they were never found they will always be suspected of doing it. The tape Norma showed me of Waldo's attempted visit to Bianca's apartment just before her death suggests that he was going to plant other items there to clinch her guilt. That means he knows where the rest of the stuff is. Anyway, that's the way it looks. And I admit I don't like it. Waldo seems a pretty decent guy.

Phil

Minutes later the reply came.

Phil

Your explanation makes no sense. He had already ensured that Bianca would be thought to be the thief. I don't think you're going to be able to separate the theft from Bianca's death. Has there been a verdict on how she died?

Roger

Waldo already thought he was under suspicion.

"Of course I am. I would suspect myself if I weren't me." He snorted through his unlit pipe.

"Do you ever smoke that thing?"

"I quit."

"You should clean it. Or get a new one."

"It wouldn't be the same."

Phil had another E-mail from Roger late that night.

Phil

What if Primero put the Newman materials in Waldo's room? Of course you'll ask why.

Roger

Roger

Why?

                                                              P.
Phil

I don't know. I'm thinking about it.

                                                         Roger

The question gave Phil a sleepless night. The following day he passed on to Swenson what Primero had told him of finding the Newman materials in Waldo's room.

"So what? Weren't they all in his charge?"

"He had reported this one missing, along with other things."

Swenson groaned. "Still that damned theft. Knight, it's not in my jurisdiction. Tell the Minneapolis police. The death occurred in Saint Paul. That's all I'm interested in."

Swenson was riding a hobby horse of his own, the possibility of death by strangulation. "But it's not a clear case."

"Why not?"

"The coroner says that if she hadn't been strangled, she would have been done in by the amount of sleeping pills in her."

"MOTHER, IT'S ALL OVER."

Dolores had reached her mother as she came off the fourth green in Tempe and wanted to talk about the birdie she had just missed making.

"There was something on the green that diverted my ball. Bird dirt or something. Otherwise . . ."

"Mother, I am not going to marry Dudley Fyte."

Maternal attention had been gained in Tempe. "Are you serious?"

"Yes."

Silence. The faint twitter of birds, busy perhaps assuring the diversion of future putts.

"I'll call you back. Are you at work?"

"In my apartment."

"At this time of day?"

"Mother . . ."

"Stay put. I'll call."

But not before she finished nine holes, and changed, and was on her way home, cussing her way through Arizona traffic.

"Now what is this all about?"

"The wedding is off."

A humming pause. "Well, we'll lose the deposit at The Morris Inn."

"Don't you want to know why?"

"I'm not sure." Mrs. Torre felt that she had earned the relative tranquillity of her widowed years. Troubles sufficient she had known, but she had outlived or outgrown them all and now wanted to head into the sunset untroubled by the slings and arrows of others' outrageous fortune, even her daughter's. She had risen to the mandatory level of excitement at the prospect of planning the wedding. Whatever her disappointment, she would not brood.

"First, I learned that he'd had an affair with a married woman, an older woman, a woman almost your age."

A philosophical sigh accompanied by car horns. "Men," Mrs. Torre said. It might have been the beginning of a long disquisition but pronounced as she pronounced it it already said everything. "You must not expect perfection, Dolores."

"I wouldn't call *not* having an affair with an older woman perfection, Mother."

"*My* age?"

"More or less. She was rebuilt several times. But now she's dead. Murdered. And Dudley is a suspect."

"My God. Of course you can't marry him. Did he do it?"

"Even if he didn't . . ."

"Of course not. I will call The Morris Inn as soon as I get home. I'm late for lunch."

Dolores had imagined a very different conversation. But it was rare that she had her mother's complete attention. Did anyone ever have anyone's full attention? Life is a pattern of interruptions: bird dirt on the putting green of life.

Dolores was staying away from the office because she could not bear to watch Dudley putting a brave face on his ambiguous situation. She could bear even less the realization that everyone at Kunert and Skye seemed to have known about Dudley and Bianca.

What a fool they must have taken her for. What a fool Dudley had taken her for. Could she have gotten through this if Larry weren't in Minneapolis? He was so bright and good and naive; how could she have preferred Dudley to him?

Now, in the light of what had happened to Bianca, in the light of the fact that Dudley was being questioned by the police about Bianca, the death, her engagement to him had become impossible. Not that she could imagine him doing harm to Bianca.

From her front window, she had a distant view of Lake Harriet, surrounded by trees so thick they seemed to form a wreathe. I am twenty-five years old, she told herself. I am young and at the beginning of my career. She felt like crying. Her triumph of the other day when she had presented the new database to the firm seemed hollow in her present mood. At the time Dudley had stood by, her patron and protector, certainly her number-one cheerleader in the firm. But the other junior partners had been sincerely grateful for her presentation. Why could she derive so little confidence from the memory? Is that what her life would be? Ups and downs at the office until she faded into retirement? She thought of her engagement to Larry and then she did cry. Sweet tears, sad tears, tears for yesteryear and youth. How young they had been. Imagine, showing up at Sacred Heart and making a reservation for a wedding six years in the future.

Now Larry and his fiancée could claim the date, the little wrinkle in their plans smoothed over because Dolores Torre had broken another engagement.

She hadn't told Dudley yet, but he could hardly be surprised. She had been stupid to let him charm away her suspicions when the painting from Bianca arrived in his office and she and Amy had opened it. Bianca had made it clear that it was not just a painting. It turned out that it commemorated the day she and Dudley had met, and she expected Dudley to hang it on his wall?

Would Dudley be able to survive the difficulties into which he had fallen? For a member of Kunert and Skye to be suspected of murder was fatal to a career, certainly it would be if he were actually indicted. Would that jeopardize his law licence? Involuntarily, she felt a pang of sympathy for him. The poor silly fool. He should have seen what kind of woman Bianca was, but of course men don't see, or, if they do, act foolishly anyway. No doubt Dudley thought he could play with fire and then withdraw when he wished, but he had reckoned without Bianca's desperation. After all, how many other such men could she have hoped to attract?

That Dudley was attractive—physically, professionally—there was little doubt. It was his character that was deficient. He was self-centered, essentially egoistic, but then few men are not. Where had she picked up such lore? It had the flavor of her mother's outlook. Dolores almost regretted having made the call to Tempe. Her mother would cancel the preparations at Notre Dame. Should she stop her?

But she sat as if without will or purpose. Larry had gone back to South Bend. She felt so alone. When the phone rang, she just stared at it, counting the rings. It would be her mother. She would call again. But then the prospect of a sympathetic voice caused her to lunge for the phone.

"Hello, Mom."

"Dolores, this is Dudley."

26 KUNERT AND SKYE HAD CALLED
him in, separately, polite, receptive, wanting
to hear what he had to tell them.

"Your side of the story," Kunert had said.

He toughed out those interviews, but those were head-on questions that could be answered. Not many others had the right or desire to question him face-to-face. But he could feel the judgment going against him in the firm; nobody had to say anything. Dolores had called in sick and was taking several days off. All he got was a busy signal when he tried to reach her. But it was too much to have Amy acting funny.

"Let's hang that picture," he said to her, his voice too hearty.

"The one that . . ."

"The beach scene with mother and daughter. I love that painting. I don't want it leaning against the wall until after the wedding."

Would Amy pass on the word that he was unchanged, chipper, full of beans, whatever? But behind the closed door of his office, he sat at his desk and brooded. The investigation of Bianca's death was in the hands of the Saint Paul police, an advantage; the local rag wasn't covering a death in Highland Village, even if they couldn't make up their mind about the cause of death. How in hell could they even hesitate? Philip Knight had described the half-empty bottles of pills found on Bianca's bed. Wouldn't they have discovered all that gunk in her during the autopsy?

He tried Dolores's number again. No luck. She had the phone off the hook. Or was she on line? She was dodging him; why kid himself? He thought of the reasons he had provided her for breaking their engagement. Bianca Primero! He had felt only relief that Bianca was dead. Never once had he felt sorrow or regret. Apart from lovemaking, she was a pretty terrible person. In the beginning, Dudley had been fascinated by her. She had money and leisure enough to do anything she damned well pleased. It seemed a definition of heaven, what everyone really wanted. But, close up, it had looked more like hell than heaven. Bianca had been bored stiff. He himself had been a means to alleviate that boredom, a diversion, a toy.

But then why wouldn't she let him go? She could go on a cruise, take her pick of dozens of men who would be happy to ease her fretful hours. Young, middle-aged, whatever. So why didn't she just let go of Dudley Fyte? There was still something like pride to be derived from the realization that she could not let him go. Lighthearted affairs with nobody hurt and no lingering claims on the parties were the stuff of myth. Real people get involved. How long had he known Bianca? How much of that time had been spent in bed? A minuscule amount. He had put up with all the rest for the sake of that. Her idea of foreplay was to assert her hold over him. Dolores had become her instrument of torture. Even while he jumped through Bianca's hoops, practically begging her to leave Dolores alone, he was dying to go down the hall with her to the bedroom.

It seemed to him now that it would have been easy to break off with Bianca. What could she tell Dolores that Dolores did not already know? Dolores had learned the worst and that had not shaken her. Now that Bianca was dead it was detectives wanting to talk to him about Bianca that had proved to be too much for Dolores.

He reached out his hand and punched redial but without hope.

"Hello, Mom."

"Dolores, this is Dudley."

A long silence. And then the receiver was eased back into the cradle.

27

➤ "LARRY HAS CHANGED," NANCY said.

Roger Knight looked at her in bewilderment. "Changed? Of course he's changed. We all do, constantly. Mobile beings, Aquinas called us, everything on earth."

"That isn't what I meant."

Roger feared he knew what she meant, but he was not the one for her to talk about such things with. She needed a wise, old, married person or a priest who had heard it all. But despite his denial of knowledge in such matters, Roger had noticed the change in Larry since his return from Minneapolis. But what Larry had said to him was more significant than anything he might have noticed.

"Coming back to campus after being in Minneapolis is weird."

"Having recently made the same transition, I haven't the least idea what you mean."

Larry had looked in the door of Roger's office in Decio and been waved in. "I've been sitting here waiting to be distracted."

"I'm not much of a distraction."

"I will be the judge of that."

Shortly afterward had come the strange remark contrasting Minneapolis and Notre Dame.

"What I mean is that, in Minneapolis I felt like an adult; and now that I'm back on campus again, I almost feel like a freshman."

"Psychologists probably have a name for that."

"What does it mean?"

"I said that they had a name for it, not that they understood it. Take a reverse analogy. A young man leaves home and goes out into the world and is a great success. He returns to his native town, and as he crosses the city limits all the experience and authority he has acquired seem to melt away and he is once more the raw, young man who left some years ago."

"That's something like it. When I come back here now I really do feel that I'm an undergraduate again."

"Ah, the nostalgia of alumni."

"That was before I met Nancy."

That was all he said, but Roger detected a good deal more, more than he wished to go into with Larry. But he had felt fear for Nancy. And now she was voicing that fear.

"A week or so away and he came back almost a stranger."

"Hardly that."

"I wonder if he still thinks of Dolores Torre."

"The girl he was engaged to marry?"

"Whose fiancé is in big trouble."

Larry had told her of the death of Bianca Primero. He would have been in Minneapolis when her body was found. Had he talked with Dolores about that? Such a tragedy could provide an occasion to erase the years since Larry and Dolores had been undergraduates together.

Roger had been brooding on the fact that the missing Newman materials had not been found in Bianca's apartment. It occurred to him that, if they had ever been in the apartment, they would have been there when he and Philip had called on Bianca about the theft from her husband's collection. She had shown little sense of the significance of the loss.

"What on earth difference does it make whether you have a first edition or the latest?" Bianca had asked.

"The content is the same of course. But, ah, the associations . . ."

She had made an angry noise. "Joseph lives too much in the past."

It was difficult not to see that as an allusion to the lost child. Joseph's long-suffering must have been a difficult cross for Bianca to bear, a constant reminder that he held her responsible for the death of their child. Of course Joseph would deny that he thought that, but didn't his whole manner toward Bianca say otherwise? No wonder she had seen his marvelous collection as a substitute for the life they could have had together?

Roger did not doubt Phil when he reported that the missing items were not in her apartment. Of course this was to accept the findings of the police, but why should they be doubted? It had to be assumed that the search had been thorough. So where were they?

- Waldo claimed to have seen Bianca and her boyfriend cruising past the house on Lake of the Isles several times. On this basis, Bianca was a prime suspect.
- But Bianca was dead, and suspicion should turn on Dudley Fyte.
- But his involvement in the theft depended on the truth of Waldo's story.
- And even if Waldo's story of Bianca and Fyte cruising past the house was true, it did not follow that they were the thieves. Maybe she was just showing him the place, and he returned alone to take an untutored look at it.
- Joseph Primero seemed convinced that his own custodian had stolen the materials.
- Waldo had removed some Newman items from the library to his room, something strictly *verboten.*

- More important. Waldo admitted to sending some Newman letters to Notre Dame, hoping to throw suspicion on Bianca.
- If one took Waldo's word throughout, the place to look for the missing items would be wherever Dudley Fyte lived.
- The list of missing items Phil had found in the wastebasket in Bianca's apartment suggested that Waldo could be believed.
- And why would Bianca steal from her own husband?

Roger did not trust his surmises about the relations between men and women, particularly when the man and woman were married. Could Bianca's flamboyant lifestyle and her silly liaison with Dudley Fyte have been simply a cry for Joseph's attention? And he remembered Phil's insistence on the significance of the lost child. He brought the matter up with Father Carmody.

"It is not that women are irrational," the priest said, gazing at Roger through his round spectacles, "it is simply that they have a different kind of rationality."

"That sounds like Newman."

"How so?"

"He said that it is unreasonable to think that reasonable always means the same thing."

"Exactly. People will call it intuition, but that is often a condescending description. Consider a mother with her child. Her understanding is deeper and more intimate than anything even a father can feel, too deep to be expressed in words we can understand."

"You have heard of the death of Mrs. Primero?"

The old priest nodded his head. "What kind of reasonableness would you call an act like that?"

"It depends on who did it."

Father Carmody wrinkled his nose. "Original sin is the single cause of an infinite variety of effects."

"Who said that?"

"I did."

Later Phil called with surprising news. "Waldo Hermes has disappeared."

28

NOTRE DAME'S HEAD ARCHIVIST wondered if the Primero Collection might not be bad luck given the recent tragic events in Minneapolis. Wendy had not yet heard of the disappearance of Waldo Hermes, curator of the collection, and Greg Whelan did not volunteer the information. If she thought the collection was ill-fated, further apparent proof of that was not needed. Besides, Whelan felt a professional solidarity with Waldo Hermes and refused to think that his disappearance meant anything beyond a desire to get away from an increasingly complicated situation—get away temporarily, that is. Whelan could not believe that Waldo himself was the thief.

"Why steal and send off to Notre Dame things that were already in his possession?" he asked Roger Knight, who had given him the news about Waldo's disappearance.

"Avert suspicion from himself? Or maybe he thought it would help Joseph Primero."

Greg remembered Waldo's account of the strained relations between the Primeros and both Roger's guesses sounded plausible.

"Of course, it was very stupid of him to run off."

"If he did," Greg said loyally.

"Good point! Just what I suggested Phil consider. Running off looks like an admission of guilt. But perhaps something has happened to him."

Here was a sobering thought. Bianca Primero was only a name to Greg Whelan, but he had sat and talked face-to-face with Waldo

Hermes and could only be upset by the thought that he, like Bianca Primero, was dead.

"Roger, what is going on? Surely you've formed some notion about what has happened in Minneapolis."

And so he had. As a matter of fact, he had formed several notions.

"There are two, perhaps related, perhaps unrelated events: the theft of items from the Primero Collection and the murder of Bianca Primero. Who might have done one or both?"

And Roger went systematically through the possible answers to that question.

"Our guiding question must be *cui bono?* Who benefits from one or both of these deeds? Let us begin with what may seem the most far-fetched, Larry Morton."

"Larry Morton!"

Roger lifted a pudgy hand. "Greg, consider this as a logical exercise, something just between ourselves. I speak to you as I do to Philip."

"Go on."

"Larry managed to combine a visit to the firm that has hired him and a confrontation with Dolores Torre about the wedding reservation at Sacred Heart Basilica. His best-laid plans have suddenly 'gang a-gley' because his former fiancée has claimed the reservation they made in both their names. Of course that is precisely what Larry intended to do himself, and that perhaps made him even angrier. In Minneapolis he meets and instantly dislikes Dudley Fyte. While Larry is still in Minneapolis, things begin to unravel between Dolores and Dudley. Larry, seeing that the discovery of the affair with Bianca was insufficient to bring Dolores to her senses, decides to do something that will implicate Dudley and remove him from the scene."

"Kill Bianca?"

"I said this was the most far-fetched hypothesis. Of course it is grounded on the assumption that Larry is once more drawn to Dolores and has more in mind than simply freeing her from Dudley."

Whelan shook his head. "Far-fetched does not begin to describe that explanation."

"Perhaps not. But there are other explanations. There is Dolores herself. A woman scorned. She has been humiliated by the information that her fiancé is still carrying on an affair with an older woman. Bianca takes her out to lunch and taunts her. She is publicly embarrassed when a very expensive painting is delivered to Dudley's office, courtesy of Bianca. She decides to put an end to the woman."

"And spirits herself into her apartment and strangles her."

"We are only discussing motive now. Opportunity is a separate issue."

"What about Dudley Fyte?"

"Of course. But he is the most obvious suspect, and for that reason, perhaps, the least likely. Of course he has motive to rid himself of this pesky woman who threatens his career and his future happiness."

"He also has opportunity."

"Yes, yes. But we are postponing consideration of that. As for motive, Dudley would seem to have the strongest. You and I can imagine the witnesses from his office, from Bianca's condo, from places where the couple have gone, all testifying to the volatile relationship between the older woman and the younger man. A prosecutor would salivate at the possibility of prosecuting Dudley. Perhaps one already is."

"Has he been arrested?"

"It is only a matter of time. And so we come to our friend Waldo."

"I have already thought of that." And Greg stated the case that could be made against the curator of the Primero Collection. It dismayed him that it sounded stronger when spoken than when he'd merely thought about it. He remembered the letters he had hidden beneath his desk blotter for several days. He'd had the sense of physically forcing himself to put them with the other items that had been sent to the Archives from Minneapolis. Of course Waldo could have surrendered to temptation.

"Good, good," Roger said.

"But I don't think he did it!"

"Next we come to Joseph Primero. Who has a longer and deeper grievance against Bianca than he? She has sullied his name, defied him with her misbehavior, set herself up as a merry widow while still his wife. And there are earlier and deeper reasons for resentment. Under his calm exterior, he must have thought many times of avenging himself on that dreadful woman."

"It is all very well to ignore opportunity, Roger, but in the end that is decisive, particularly if they all have a motive, however farfetched. And you have divorced the murder from the theft of those items from the collection. But surely they are connected."

"Connected they are, but were they the acts of the same person? Take comfort from that thought, Greg. Our friend Waldo Hermes might be responsible for the missing items and have had nothing to do with Bianca's death."

Late that night, as Greg Whelan sat sipping beer and reading Trollope's *Kept in the Dark*, there was an urgent knock on the door of his apartment. He froze in his chair. The outer door of the building in which he lived was left unlocked so that the doors of apartments were the first and last bastion against undesired callers. Greg sat still. He thought of turning off the light, then did. The knock came again. He rose slowly from his chair and crept toward the door; focused light streamed through the peephole. He moved to one side to avoid a sofa he could not see and banged into the coffee table, sending things clattering onto the floor. He remained still, his shin throbbing with pain, and listened, hoping the caller would go away. And then he heard his name whispered on the other side of the door.

When he put his eye to the viewer, he saw a stranger standing there, a bald stranger who bore a resemblance to a frog. The face came closer.

"Whelan, it's me, Waldo Hermes!"

Greg opened the door and Waldo stumbled into the darkened room. Greg threw the switch beside the door and turned to look at his visitor. It was all he could do not to laugh. Waldo Hermes had shaved off his beard and shaved as well the hair from his head so that only the thick thatch of his eyebrows relieved the doughy expanse of his face.

"Would you recognize me?" Waldo asked anxiously.

"Why did you run away?"

"I'll tell you everything. Do you have anything to eat?"

It would have been too much to say that the shaven Waldo Hermes was an aesthetic improvement over the natural hairy version of the man; but once the initial shock was over, Greg found it almost possible to ignore what the curator had done to himself by way of disguise.

"How often do you have to shave?"

"My face?"

"No, your head."

What used to be called five o'clock shadow relieved the bareness of the curator's pate.

"Just once a day. I have to shave my face twice a day. That's why I grew a beard in the first place."

"Now tell me what has happened."

29 ———→ THE   DISAPPEARANCE   OF
Waldo Hermes bothered the police more
than it did Joseph Primero.

"He is not under contract to me. He has always been free to go
whenever he wanted to."

"Did he say good-bye?"

Primero smiled at Phil Knight. Knight was his employee too, at
least for the nonce, but he did not think that the private investigator
would skedaddle to South Bend without letting him know.

"Not all employees are equally sensitive."

Swenson asked, "Does that mean you're offended by his departure?"

What a tiresome thing a police investigation is. There had been a
lull during the period of the wake and funeral, but on the way back
from the cemetery Primero was accompanied by Swenson, who
wanted a few words.

"Lieutenant, my wife is dead. Someone killed her. How are you
going to find that someone by asking me questions?"

"Do you own the building in which your wife lived."

"The condominium? I built it."

"Are you still the owner."

"I am a partner."

"So your wife paid no rent."

"I took care of that."

"Isn't that unusual?"

"For a husband to pay his wife's expenses?"

Swenson fell silent and watched the world through the tinted windows of the funeral director's limousine. O'Dell, the undertaker, sat in front next to the driver. He was still disappointed that he had been unsuccessful in persuading Primero to have a miniature replica of Saint Peter's built to house the remains of his wife. Was Swenson his revenge?

"Have you arrested Dudley Fyte yet, Lieutenant?"

"No."

"I hope he doesn't leave town."

"He's been told not to."

"Well, that should suffice."

By the time the sarcasm hit Swenson, they were pulling into O'Dell's parking lot. Philip Knight was already there, waiting. He was surprised to see Swenson emerge from the undertaker's limousine.

"I'm not under arrest," Primero said to Phil Knight.

"What did you mean about Dudley Fyte?" Swenson asked.

"If he's your man, you'd better take him into custody."

Phil went with Primero to the house where they talked about the investigation.

"You're right, Joseph. They ought to move on Dudley."

"You think he did it?"

"Well, God knows he had motive enough." Phil then proceeded to convey to Joseph the contents of an E-mail he had received from his brother listing the motives of the people connected with Bianca.

"He really thinks I myself might have done it?"

"This is all abstract. Algebraic. Quite impersonal. And, as Roger notes, the question of opportunity has not been raised."

"It's odd even to be speculated about."

"There is also the gate guard of the condominium, a tough little bird named Norma. She could be of help."

"How so?"

"She sees a lot and remembers a lot, but her memory is supplemented by the monitors in the security system."

Primero nodded. "To increase her field of vision."

"And record it."

"She told you that?"

"And showed me some samples. Swenson doesn't know about it yet, but he soon will. Then he can assign people to the patient task of looking at hours and days and weeks of film in which by and large absolutely nothing happens."

But it was to check Waldo's quarters that Philip Knight had come. Primero told him the police had already ransacked Waldo's little apartment over the garage of the house on Lake of the Isles. "Once I told them I had seen the *Apologia* there that later was missing altogether they couldn't wait to tear up the place."

Primero had left the police to their work, but he went up to the garage apartment with Phil and, when he entered felt even more than before like an intruder. He had worked almost daily with Hermes, but this was the area of the curator's privacy. Primero had been struck by its austerity. Waldo must have had most of the furniture removed. The outer room had a trestle table set up in its center at which Waldo had sat in a secretary's chair. He had used a similar chair in the house itself for the back support. There were no shelves, just books rising in tottering piles from the floor on three sides of the room. A lounge chair, which elongated to a supine position, was looked upon by a modernistic lamp whose light bounced off the low ceiling. The bedroom was monastic. A single bed, carefully made, a chair on one side, a small bookshelf on the other, the only light the ceiling lamp. A dresser on which a small statue of the Madonna sat. There was a crucifix on the wall over the bed. Phil opened the closet door. It had not been emptied. The bathroom was a mess, a towel lying in the basin; the bottom of the tub had hair in it.

"He must molt when he showers."

"The police concluded that he had left on the spur of the moment." Primero smiled at Phil.

The Primero Collection was kept on the first floor of the house itself, using the library and garden room and a structure that had been added to the back.

"It had been my intention to turn the whole house into a library. The thought returned after my wife left, but by then I had already made the decision to donate everything to Notre Dame. The zoning laws here ruled out my idea of course, but I think I could have won a legal battle. Such a library would enhance the neighborhood rather than the reverse."

"I wish Roger were here," said Phil.

"I could have him flown up."

"He almost never flies. And never without me."

"Is there a special reason why you want him?"

"Joseph, you've met him. He understands all this as well as your man Waldo does." Phil paused. "The question arises as to whether there is anything else missing."

Primero smiled. "I am not quite that dependent on the veracity of my employees. Every item is bar coded. The code is read by a very sensitive device. This provides me with an all but instantaneous inventory. It is how the thefts were known."

Phil wanted to telephone his brother from Waldo's desk amid the collection, so Joseph Primero left the private investigator. "The door will lock when you leave, Phil."

"You're going?"

"I have a little errand."

Phil Knight's car was parked by the garages. Joseph took the little olive-colored Mercedes convertible. Once behind the wheel, he rolled up the tinted windows, adjusted his cap in the rearview mirror, and donned oversize sunglasses. Then he purred down the driveway.

DUDLEY WAS TAKEN INTO custody in his office, where he had foolishly gone in the conviction that the police, having done nothing thus far, would continue to do nothing. Amy, his secretary, came into his office, openmouthed, followed by Swenson and a uniformed policeman.

"Dudley Fyte, you are under arrest as a suspect in the murder of Bianca Primero. You have the right to remain silent . . ."

Dudley listened to the ritualistic phrase, recited with all the solemnity of a priest by Lieutenant Swenson. Dudley became a mute. He was led out of his office and down the corridor, where colleagues came to their doors to watch him go by. This was ignominy indeed. But it was liberating as well. He might have been shucking off all the inhibitions that go with the struggle to rise in the corporate and social scale. He looked dispassionately at the shocked faces of men and women he would doubtless never see again. Whatever happened he would not return to Kunert and Skye. It was odd that being suspected of murder should exhilarate him so.

The one face he did not see on that Via Dolorosa out of Kunert and Skye was Dolores Torre's. That he could not have borne. It was to her his thoughts turned when, after being taken to downtown Saint Paul and booked, he was told he could call a lawyer. He stared silently at Swenson.

"It's all right to talk now."

Dudley said nothing.

"Is there a lawyer you would like to call?"

What power silence gave him over Swenson. He wondered if he would ever speak again. He was led to a holding cell with Swenson explaining that if he did not select a lawyer one would be assigned him.

"We're due in court at two o'clock."

Today? He almost asked it aloud. But then he was alone.

The prominence of the toilet and washbasin and bed seemed to reduce life in a cell to its animal basics. It was a setting conducive to meditation, if brooding over the events of recent weeks could be called meditation.

Ten years ago he had emerged from the law school of the University of Chicago, passed the bar exams in a breeze, and put his foot firmly on the bottom rung at Kunert and Skye. His diploma from Chicago blotted out his prehistory, the windswept little town in western Nebraska, his dirt-poor family that had a long-term relationship with bad luck, the brothers and sisters who ignored the praise with which he swept through school. He graduated a month before his seventeenth birthday and went off to Chicago to take up the scholarship he had been awarded.

"Make us proud of you," Mr. Warbke, his faculty adviser, had said.

His parents and siblings just stared him onto the bus. On the long ride to Chicago, he'd studied the list of names he had made up over the years, trying to decide who he would be. He changed his name to Dudley Fyte in his first year of law school, and it was as Dudley Fyte that he had entered the employ of Kunert and Skye, and it was as Dudley Fyte that he was arraigned before Judge Rita Callisher that afternoon.

"Cat got your tongue?" the judge asked sweetly, before assigning him a lawyer.

Back in jail he continued the review of his life. He thought of Bonner, wondering if that incident would be raised at his trial. He thought of Bianca, of that fateful meeting in the art gallery in Highland Village. He thought of the sentimental painting that she had sent him as a vindictive gift. But most of all he thought of Dolores.

Once she had accepted his proposal, he should never have looked back. She was his destiny. He might have told her about Bianca, some sanitized version that would have defanged his mistress. By trying to keep it a secret, he had made Bianca into a threat.

"Your lawyer," the guard said, unlocking his cell.

He was taken to a room where Dolores awaited him.

"Are you my lawyer?" His heart leapt. Had Kunert and Skye decided to get behind their fallen partner and provide him with all the professional help he needed.

"Dudley, you know I'm not a lawyer."

"Did they send you?"

But her expression was enough to snuff out the mad hope that he had friends and support. He was reduced to the condition that had been his as a boy in Nebraska; he began to weep.

"Oh, Dudley."

She came around the table, but he turned away although he was proud of his tears, they were so uncalculated. She put her hand on his arm. The tenderness came and went like an electric shock. He was no longer weeping when he looked at her.

"Why have you come? Because you missed my ignominious departure from Kunert and Skye?"

She stepped back, surprised at his vehemence. But she now represented something in the irredeemable past. He no longer felt anything for her. It was all gone, blown away like tumbleweed across the featureless prairie of his youth.

"Who is your lawyer?"

"They will assign me one."

"Assign you one."

"We will make a team, whoever it is. And I will win. It is no easy matter to convict an innocent man."

His chin lifted as he spoke, but he could see that nothing he could have said would have convinced her more thoroughly of his guilt.

31 "WHERE IS LARRY?" ROGER Knight asked Nancy Beatty.

"He's gone back to Minneapolis."

"Again?"

"They talked him into joining the firm right away. No reason not to. His final semester has been just odds and ends. He's already fulfilled the course requirements."

"Leaving all the wedding preparations to you."

"I guess. Maybe we'll postpone it. I could start graduate work."

"At Northwestern."

"Yes."

Of course Roger did not pursue this surprising suggestion. In any case, he had come to visit with Nancy's father, Professor Beatty, whose study at home was even more chaotic than his office in Decio. His wife was not permitted entry, she being a compulsively neat person who dreaded anyone's seeing the squalor in which her husband preferred to work.

"I'm not responsible," she said, taking Roger to the door of the study and averting her face.

"Nancy says Larry has gone back to Minneapolis," Roger whispered.

In answer, Mrs. Beatty let her eyes roll upward, a look of resignation that covered both the condition of Professor Beatty's study and her daughter's suddenly indefinite wedding plans.

Experience had taught Roger to settle for a hassock on which to sit, if one were available; his second choice was a couch he could have all to himself like La Signora in *Barchester Towers*. None of the chairs in the study could accommodate a significant fraction of him, but, *deo gratias,* there was a hassock over which he could spill in all directions. The difficulty was in rising again, but here Beatty, surprisingly strong for such a wiry little man, would be of help. Beatty closed the door with the decisiveness of an angel closing the gates of paradise and picked up his pipe. A ceiling fan rotated slowly above him, distributing the smoke evenly around the room.

"Roger, I've read Newman's letter to Trollope."

"Good for you."

"Gregory Whelan was discreetly helpful." Beatty leaned toward Roger. "I made a photocopy."

"It's too bad such a treasure came to the Archives in such an unusual way."

"The murder in Minneapolis?"

"Well, yes."

"I find it perfectly understandable."

"You do."

Beatty rapped on his knee with his pipe, about to rule. "I would have gladly wrung that woman's neck myself. Imagine, turning items like these into some kind of game. And she was a Jezebel besides. The sooner the whole kit and caboodle is out of such hands and safely in the Archives, the better." Beatty drew on his pipe as if to calm himself.

"Joseph Primero is a very different kind of person."

"He sounds like a wimp to me. Casper Milquetoast. But you wouldn't remember that. Beware of a man who lets his wife dominate him."

Professor Beatty's voice raised as he pronounced what he took to

170

be a basic truth. And sitting there in the cherished disorder of his study, he spoke with authority. No cloister could have been less subject to invasion than Professor Beatty's place of work. It did not surprise Roger that Beatty had absolutely no trouble finding things either here at home or in his office in Decio. Order is an analogous concept, not to be confused with neatness. He might have said it aloud, making an addition to Beatty's list of self-evident truths, but he turned the conversation to Nancy.

"I pray that it is over. Imagine passing up a full scholarship to graduate school to rush into marriage. I have nothing against whatchamacallit, but why hurry? Let him get settled in his profession, let her get a doctorate, then they can talk about marriage."

"It may be now or never."

"Yes," Beatty said, and his expression suggested which alternative he thought would prevail.

The following day Joseph Primero showed up at Notre Dame calling on Greg Whelan, who telephoned Roger with the news. The university benefactor was on campus.

"He's in conference with Wendy now. Can we meet at the Huddle?"

Roger drove his golf cart along the campus walks, saluting and being saluted by students as he went. What satisfaction he felt being a member of the university and having its scholarly resources at his beck and call. And the friendship of Greg Whelan was a particular bonus.

"Primero says he is ready to transfer his collection to the Archives immediately; no need to wait for the new building to go up."

Roger surveyed the array of hamburgers and french fries on the tray before him. As midday approached, the Huddle was full of undergraduates who had chosen this alternative to one of the dining halls, along with graduate students, faculty, and members of the staff. There were half a dozen other such alternative restaurants around the campus now, but the Huddle remained the most popular, a kind of town meeting place in the center of the campus where Italian food, junk food, and stir fry, as well as the deli provided for the gustatory needs of its customers. Roger and Greg occupied a booth whose benches could accommodate Roger's width, but if his north and south were taken care of, to east and west there was a tight fit because of the intervening table.

"It is not always wise to make a precipitous move after the death of a spouse."

"It is the loss of Waldo Hermes that is the proximate cause. He can't face the task of replacing him."

"I wonder where he is?"

Greg dipped a french fry in a little container of ketchup. "At my place."

"Your place!"

"He showed up the other night. I hardly recognized him. He has shaved off his beard and shaved his head as well."

"A disguise?"

"Until he identified himself, I did not know who he was."

"What does he have to say for himself?"

"He feels he is under suspicion. The worst of it is, he feels responsible for the theft of those items."

"Well, unless he stole them, he isn't."

"It is largely a professional disappointment with himself."

"Do you think he would agree to see me?"

"I promised to bring him food."

They took it together, conveying it to the despondent curator in Roger's golf cart.

The naked face of Hermes peered out at them over the security chain of Greg Whelan's door.

"Edgar G. Robinson," Roger said, when the door had been shut, the chain removed, and then opened again. Waldo Hermes had retreated out of sight. Roger's remark puzzled him.

"An actor you look like."

"I don't like the part I'm playing."

When Greg told his guest that Joseph Primero was on campus, Waldo stopped, holding the Styroform container in both hands.

"How did he know?"

"That you're here? He doesn't."

"I couldn't face him."

"Waldo," Roger said, "no one can blame you."

"I blame myself."

"I can understand that, but it is nonsense."

"No. I should have warned him that his wife had been lurking about the neighborhood."

"To steal things from the collection?"

"Obviously."

"Possibly. Dudley Fyte has been taken into custody."

"What for?"

"He is accused of killing Bianca Primero."

But murder did not rank as high as the theft of the precious items from the collection that had been in Waldo's custody, except perhaps that it provided an exculpating motive for killing the wayward wife.

"Primero says he wants to transfer his collection to the university as soon as possible."

The great naked head nodded. "A good idea. Here it will be safe."

"What will you do?"

Waldo looked sheepish. "It will seem quixotic at my age, but I want to spend time in a monastery. My destination is a Trappist monastery, New Melleray Abbey, near Dubuque."

"You want to become a monk?"

"Domine, non sum dignus. Just a long stay in the guest house."

"And then?"

"God knows. Joseph Primero has provided me with a comfortable retirement."

How old was Waldo Hermes? His age seemed even more indeterminate without the abundance of hair. Both Roger and Whelan acknowledged the attraction of a stay with the Trappist monks.

After much persuasion, Hermes agreed that he must meet with his employer, or his former employer, as he insisted. "I deserted my post. I failed in my duty." Clearly, Hermes felt more comfortable with the pangs of guilt than he would have with exoneration. Perhaps he thought seeing Primero would provide more laceration to his delicate conscience.

Greg called the Archives and arranged for a meeting with Primero at The Morris Inn, where the benefactor had taken a room. Roger got into his cart, and went to his office, where he checked his E-mail and found a message from Phil.

Roger

I told you about the security system at the condo where Mrs. Primero lived and of the taped record kept there. Of course I passed this information on to Lieutenant Swenson, but when he went to the condo with a court order he was told by Norma that the tapes had been destroyed. He is threatening legal action, claiming the destruction of materials relevant to a murder investigation. You will wonder who gave the order. All Norma would tell me was that it had been a decision by the governing board of the condominium. I wonder if Joseph Primero was consulted? He *is* a member of the board. Moreover, it turns out that he has kept a small apartment there, the builder's prerogative. It's called the penthouse, but its just a little place on the roof. Odd that Mrs. Primero did not live in it. Probably not posh enough.

P

Roger thought of telephoning Phil to discuss the message, but instead he fell into a kind of reverie. Even the most innocuous events become incredibly complicated when subjected to scrutiny. But of course few events are scrutinized, followed as they swiftly are by a continuous flow of further events.

32 IF NORMA WAS GLAD TO SEE
Philip Knight, she concealed it well.

"Oh please, not again. I've wasted too much time with you guys already."

"What guys are those?"

She meant Swenson, she meant the lab people who haunted the still marked-off apartment where Bianca Primero had died, she meant all the fuss of the murder investigation. For it was unequivocally a murder investigation now. It had been a toss-up between the pills and strangulation, and Swensen had chosen strangulation.

"One, I am a private investigator. Two, all this is meant to make life safer for young women like yourself."

"You mean women cheating on their husbands? I'm not one of those. What if she got what she deserved, and soon he will get what he deserves?"

"The murderer?"

"You know who I mean."

"You didn't exactly help when you got rid of all those tapes."

"*I* got rid of them? Did I own them? I just turned them over to the owner."

"Who requested them?"

"The one who also requested I not say, it being no one else's business."

"You are in a surly mood."

Norma lit a cigarillo and her cheeks hollowed as she inhaled. "I just don't want it to be my word that does him in."

Here was the heart of the matter. Norma had of course identified Dudley Fyte as the young man who had been the dead woman's lover. "It was public knowledge! Any number of people could tell you the same thing."

But not everyone could place Dudley at the apartment on the crucial day. Not everyone knew that although he had to go through the gate and thus past her if he drove, he could walk to the main door unassisted and unseen and let himself in.

"Anyone with a key could do that. But I didn't know they had found keys on him."

The keys had been found in the glove compartment of Dudley's car. There had been a key to the front door of the building and a key to the apartment, plus other still unidentified keys.

"So how could you testify that he had been here that day?"

"I couldn't. He signed the visitor's book in the foyer."

This was true. The visitor's book, placed on a little lectern with a stainless steel pen chained to it, was more ignored than used. But on the day before the body of Bianca was discovered, there was Dudley's name in the book, time of arrival, time of departure. The time span covered the estimated time of death of Bianca. And there were several earlier such entries that could be consulted for comparison. The same signature in all cases.

"So it doesn't rest on your word."

"They say I will be called upon to testify. The prosecutor has been here."

The prosecutor, a young hotshot named Jack Cousey, spoke of his case with all the cocky enthusiasm of someone who thirsted for fame as much as justice.

"Tight as a drum," he described his case. "But any case can be screwed up. That is why it was given to me."

"To screw it up?"

"I may call you as a witness."

Phil laughed. "Witness to what?"

"Oh, come on. Primero hired you." Cousey frowned. "Why have you stuck around?"

"I was hired to investigate a theft of books from his home on Lake of the Isles."

"As opposed to his little pied à terre in the condo in Highland Village? In my jurisdiction." Another frown. He seemed to frown whenever he was diverted from touting himself. "The theft's been solved, hasn't it?"

"The mystery is lifting."

"What the hell does that mean?"

"I don't know who the thief is yet."

He meant "know" as in know for certain beyond the shadow of a doubt. Roger had told him that the shaven Hermes—the depilated god, as Roger called him—had shown up at Notre Dame. Joseph Primero was also there.

"And I am here in snowy exile, forced to watch the Irish play basketball on television."

The men's team was at last equaling the feats of the Notre Dame women's basketball team. After the football team lost its bowl game, any Notre Dame victory in any sport restored the wounded pride of Irish fans. But basketball victories were salve indeed.

"Roger, are you sure Waldo isn't our thief?"

There was a long pause during which Roger seemed to be humming a Gregorian chant. "Yes."

"You're sure."

"Wasn't that the question?"

"You are sure Waldo Hermes did not steal those items from the Primero Collection?"

"I am sure of that."

"What *aren't* you sure of?"

"That natural events can ever be as precise as mathematical formulae. There may be as yet unknown but relevant objections to proofs of God's existence . . ."

Phil's only defense was to sing *La Marseillaise,* off key.

When Roger was in an enigmatic mood, he was hard to shake into clarity face-to-face, but Phil knew it was a losing cause over the telephone. He was in an annoyed and perplexed mood when he hung up and tried to settle down for an evening of televised pro basketball. What was he still doing in the Twin Cities? Everyone else had deserted the place and Roger was down in South Bend imagining possible accounts of what had happened in Bianca Primero's condo. Unable to concentrate as one must in order truly to enjoy a game, he gave up and went downtown to headquarters, where Swenson, almost as smug as Cousey, was happy to go through the case he had built for the prosecutor.

"It's classic stuff, Knight. Young man hooks up with older woman, in this case one who still had a husband. Who can understand the motive in such cases? It doesn't matter. Fyte admits he had an affair with her. Others know about it. The gate guard of the condo knew about his visits there. Everything is just fine until he wants to unload the old doll. But she isn't ready to say quits. Fyte has fallen for a young coworker; they are talking marriage. But Mrs. Primero intervenes. She embarrasses Fyte. There is only one way to get her off his back."

"Murder her."

"That's right."

"Sounds good."

"And you know something? I don't have to mention the theft, or alleged theft, of any books."

"I want to talk to him."

Swenson shrugged. "Why not?"

Adversity had stripped Fyte of the veneer of self-assurance Phil had found offensive before. Humbled, the lawyer accepted Phil's visit as if he himself had no say in anything anymore.

"There's no point in asking me any questions when my lawyer isn't present."

"Do you want to call him?"

"Not really."

"Besides, you're a lawyer yourself."

"But I don't have a fool for a client."

He meant himself. "My interest is not the murder of Bianca Primero. What did you know of Joseph Primero's rare book collection?"

"Only what Bianca told me."

"What did she tell you?"

"Mainly what a nut her husband was about musty old books you couldn't get rid of at a garage sale."

"Actually, they are very valuable."

"She said he loved those books more than anything, more than her."

"Did she ever show you any of the books?"

"How could she do that?"

"Never had any of them in her apartment?"

"I told you, she hated those books. Why would she want them around her?"

"I was hired by Joseph Primero to find who had stolen things from his collection. Some items showed up at the Notre Dame Archives, which is destined to get the collection eventually. But the rest are missing, including a very valuable first edition of the *Apologia* of Cardinal Newman. It is not at the house on Lake of the Isles. They are not in the Archives at Notre Dame. So where are they?"

"You're going to tell me."

"I was hoping you would tell me."

"What in hell does all this have to do with me?"

"A great deal. You went to the house on Lake of the Isles with a list Bianca had prepared for you. What did you do with the books after you took them from the house?"

"Where do you get such fantasies."

Phil took out his wallet and opened it, showing Dudley the now smoothed slip of paper he had taken from the wastebasket in Bianca's apartment. Dudley looked at it closely.

"That's her handwriting."

"The note also has fingerprints on it. There are more fingerprints in the house on Lake of the Isles. Among your keys was one to that house."

He had suggested fantasies, so Phil gave him fantasies. If Dudley had handled this slip of paper, perhaps his prints could be found on it. If he had been inside the house on Lake of the Isles to take those books, more prints should be discoverable there. And Swensen had mentioned yet to be identified keys in Fyte's possession.

"Is that what you came to tell me?"

"More or less."

"Can I tell you something now?"

"Go ahead."

Dudley Fyte leaned across the little table separating the two men. He looked intently into Philip's eye, but his lip trembled and it was a moment before he spoke. "Even if all that you said were true, I did not kill her, Knight. Please believe me. No one else does, but somebody has to. I am innocent."

Phil showed the poor devil such sympathy as he could. When has an accused murderer failed to proclaim his innocence? Maybe it all seemed a bad dream now and Fyte really believed he had not done what he did. He was led away but before disappearing he flung one last pleading look at Phil.

33 ➤ "WHAT ARE YOU GOING TO do?" Larry Morton asked Dolores. They were in a bar on Grand Avenue with a pitcher of sangria before them. The music was insistently South of the Border, either jangling and jumpy or Lenten and tragic.

"Consulting? 'The last refuge of the scoundrel.' " She turned her glass as if in search of true north. "I still have these phrases and sayings that I picked up as a student. I don't even remember the name of the class or who the professor was. 'To understand is to forgive.' "

"Madame De Stael."

"How did you know that?"

"It was in the crossword puzzle yesterday. No, I just remember. It was the one we called Pom Pom."

"For pomposity. He taught English."

Silence. Memories. So long ago. Notre Dame. "Of course, it's not distant to you, Larry. You've been there all along."

"Arrested something or other."

"Sometimes I wish I'd never left."

That could have happened, of course. The two of them married, he in law school, she too, if that's what she wanted. An apartment in married student housing, if they could get one, where fecundity was the order of the day. Or night. He looked away. "Why did we break up exactly?"

He pretended it was just a question asked in the interests of historical accuracy. Getting it straight. Dispassionate. But how in the present circumstances could it be that for either of them? Dolores sat upright and open faced across from him, a picture of self-possession, young woman on the go. Yet he could feel her straining toward him across the table just as he felt drawn to her. First love is indelible. He tried to think of Nancy and found he couldn't.

She tipped her head to one side at his question. Her eyes lifted and she looked above and beyond him. She shrugged.

"Remember the day we went over to Sacred Heart and made the reservation?"

That broke the dam holding back the memories. They vied with one another to recall in as minute detail as possible things they had done half a dozen years ago and more, where they had gone, their friends, nightly visits to the Grotto, where they'd knelt side by side as if in anticipation of their wedding day. His hand went out for hers, and they seemed to pull one another closer across the table. Her face leaned toward his. And then, after an electric silence, she sat back.

"I guess I wanted more than seemed to be in prospect. Well, I sure got more, didn't I?"

"Look at it this way. You were saved by the bell. What if you had learned all this stuff after . . ."

"I told you that she actually asked me to lunch? Bianca Primero? We met in Dayton's Tea Room. My fiancé's mistress. A minor version of *The Golden Bowl*."

"Did Notre Dame play in that one?"

"Pom Pom again."

"He was cheerleader. We played Southern Cal."

She took his hands and squeezed, and her face was close to his again. He leaned forward until the tips of their noses touched. They remained like that for minutes.

"We've become eskimos."

"Stuck in our igloo."

"Epoxy."

Her head turned, pivoting on her nose, and then his lips slid onto hers. The table between them might have been the moral law. She sat back slowly, her eyes closed. "What about Nancy?"

"I don't know."

Meaning, of course, that he did. The only question was how he was to tell her. One thing he and Dolores would have in common was two broken engagements. That was two things. But sitting with her in the booth in the bar on Grand Avenue he did not believe that there had ever been any break in what they had first felt for one another long ago at Notre Dame.

"I'll talk to her."

"Oh, Larry." But she was thinking more of Nancy than she was of him. At least Dudley had had the grace to commit murder and be taken out of the picture.

They sat on, conscious that the main issue had been settled; they were once again a couple. No need to think now of the next step, but how could either of them forget that reservation at the Basilica of the Sacred Heart for June 17?

PART THREE

34 ⇢ PHIL FLEW IN FROM MIN-
neapolis—via Chicago, of course—and that
night Roger made goulash and a huge salad. Their guests were
Father Carmody, Greg Whelan, and Waldo Hermes. While they ate,
the television, muted, brought in the Notre Dame/Seton Hall game,
but only Phil paid any attention to it. His sudden grunts and groans,
cheers and curses, might have alarmed anyone who thought he was
reacting to things said at the table. Roger had already debriefed his
brother during the drive from the airport, Greg Whelan behind the
wheel of the vehicle that had been specially adapted to the trans-
porting of Roger Knight.

"The prosecutor is confident of a guilty verdict," Phil said.

"When is the trial?"

"Next month."

"What did Dudley say to you when you saw him?"

"That he was innocent of course."

"I suppose this breaks his engagement."

Philip did not understand.

"His engagement to the woman Larry Morton broke his engagement to."

"Dolores Torre. That's right."

"When did you last talk with her?"

Philip was not sure. He had not talked to her recently, that was
clear. But these events must have completely upset her life. Roger
doubted that she would continue to be engaged to Dudley Fyte,

guilty or innocent. His offenses against her were not in the criminal code. Would she be drawn back to Larry, proximity doing what proximity often does in such cases? An image of magnets and steel filings came to him and he winced. Avoid metaphor. The literal is poetic enough, poetry being both comic and tragic.

"Phil, do you think that Fyte killed that woman?"

"Don't you?"

"You have been much closer to everything."

"Finding the stolen items in a briefcase stashed in the trunk of Bianca's Jaguar pretty well seals it, Roger."

"No doubt about it being Fyte's briefcase?"

"Fingerprints all over it." Suddenly Phil grinned. "Did I tell you what I said to Fyte about fingerprints?"

He had spoken as if the discovery was already made—Fyte's fingerprints on the list Phil had retrieved from Bianca's wastebasket, Fyte's fingerprints in the library of the house on Lake of the Isles. A key to that house on Fyte's key ring.

"I was wrong only about the slip of paper. Well, not wrong. The results were inconclusive."

"When will the police turn over the Newman materials?"

"They already have." Phil nodded toward the luggage he had tossed into the back of the van. "When did you ever know me to carry a briefcase."

"So your job is done."

"Two birds with one stone."

He meant the theft from Primero's collection and the death of Bianca Primero.

"If the verdict of murder sticks."

"What do you mean?"

"A case can be made that it was the pills she swallowed rather than the strangling that killed her. Someone in the Coroner's Office is making that case and threatens to go public. There could be a Solomonian decision, Roger."

"Neither/nor?"

"Both/and. Or maybe it will be either/or/or."

"Where does Solomon come in?"

"Asphyxiation, without specifying whether due to strangling or not."

"Dudley Fyte must be going crazy wondering if there is a crime for him to be accused of."

Now at table, if Phil was distracted by the fortunes of the televised game, Roger found himself mentally picking away at the account he had gotten from Philip. But Greg and Waldo were in no need of conversational catalyst. Cohabitation had made them friends as well as respected colleagues. Waldo might have been trying to get himself all talked out before he went off for his stay with the Trappists. The topic was the extent of Cardinal Newman's interest in Trollope, triggered by the letter from the Primero Collection.

"Did you ever read Newman's novel?" Father Carmody asked Roger.

"Didn't he write two?"

"Not unless you count the one I read as a novel. Dull as sin."

Roger did not pursue the matter. Besides, Carmody was trying unsuccessfully to divide his attention between the table conversation and the basketball game. The priest, never having seen Waldo in his natural hairy condition, was seemingly less struck by the nakedness of his head and face.

"Odd that a man with eyebrows like that should be bald," he had whispered to Roger earlier.

"He read too much Occam." Unforgiveable, but Father Carmody either failed to hear it or ignored the terrible joke.

Notre Dame lost in the final seconds and for a time gloom settled over half the table. Greg was going on about the poetry of Patrick Cavanaugh, when he became aware that he had everyone's attention. Immediately his stammer silenced him. But Waldo picked up the ball: Ireland, New Melleray, a reference to Joyce's *The Dead*. His own prospective withdrawal to the rural fastness of Iowa, where silence was as golden as the corn. Father Carmody spoke of members of the congregation who had felt drawn to the Trappists.

"Came back like a serve in tennis, most of them." He held out his glass, and Phil poured it full of red wine. "Do you know the story of Father Hudson?"

They were going to hear it in any case; it was one of Father Carmody's set pieces. Hudson had been on a train bound for the Trappists and Father Sorin was on the same train. The founder of Notre Dame explained to the young man what was happening in northern Indiana and how his vocation might more fittingly be answered there. When Sorin got off the train at South Bend, so did young Hudson. Later, ordained, he ran *Ave Maria* magazine and published many good and bad nineteenth-century authors.

Phil was tired from his journey, Greg and Waldo could continue their conversation more fluently at Greg's apartment, and Father Carmody was openly yawning, as if his reminiscing had spelled the end of the evening.

"You should have invited Joseph Primero, Roger."

"I did. He declined. He wants us for lunch at The Morris Inn tomorrow."

"How is he holding up?"

"Fussing about the transfer of his collection keeps his mind off his loss."

Roger seldom had sleepless nights, but that night was one of them. The pans were washed, the dishes were in the washer, everything spick and span, so the thought of the morning's housekeeping did not explain his wakefulness.

Waldo Hermes's intention to spend a prolonged stay in the Trappist guesthouse at New Melleray in Iowa might have suggested a troubled conscience, a guilty soul off to make expiation for some dreadful deed. The moral and legal orders are very different. Repentance and confession could suffice for a theft, with no further obligation if the deed did not do a great injustice to the bereaved. There was little that could have been done to compensate Joseph Primero for the loss of Bianca. The real loss had antedated her death by years. But remorse and penance would have continued after confession; and Waldo, if he were Bianca's murderer, would have been incapable of simply going on as before. So off to the monastery.

Roger's dismissive snort at his own thoughts was audible. A man as morally sensitive as this imagined Waldo could hardly have allowed Dudley Fyte to pay for his deed. And so, in the dead of night, he studied his wild cards. Larry first, who could remove the obstacle to his refound love for Dolores by setting him up for a murder charge. Or Dolores herself, irked by the condescension of Dudley's mistress in Dayton's Tea Room, visits her apartment and . . . Sleep came at last, overwhelming such unlikely thoughts. He never even made it to Joseph Primero.

35

SORIN'S, THE RESTAURANT in The Morris Inn, was crowded, but Joseph Primero had wisely made a reservation when he'd dined there the previous night.

"It's why I couldn't join in your welcome home party," he said to Philip.

"Is that what it was?"

They were at a table near the window, with the residence halls that had been built on the former golf course crowding the sky. Father Carmody's reminder that it had once been a pasture and had served other functions before becoming a golf course did not lessen the pain of alumni and senior faculty who had played the course in the dim, dark days beyond recall.

Joseph Primero was natty in a blue blazer with very golden buttons and pale gray slacks that added to the nautical effect. An ascot was stuffed into his unbuttoned shirt. He tasted fastidiously of his spinach salad.

"People speak of the special atmosphere of this university," he said. "It's true. I attended Mass in the Basilica at eleven-thirty this morning. One of the officers of the university said the Mass and gave a homily that lasted maybe four or five minutes. Simple, lucid, edifying."

The previous night, Primero had braved the icy walks of the campus and gone down below the Basilica to the Grotto, where the blaze of devotional candles brought home to him the university's dedication to Our Lady.

" 'Notre Dame' becomes like 'Los Angeles.' People forget what it means."

He had also walked down the road toward Saint Mary's College but had not gone far. He wanted to save that for the daytime.

"Where will the site of the new Archives building be?" Phil asked.

"That is not for me to decide of course. The Holy Cross Province Archives is back on Douglas Road, near the seminary. Perhaps not central enough for the University Archives."

"Has there ever been any thought of Waldo Hermes coming here with the collection?"

This idea had of course crossed Primero's mind in the past, when the transfer of the collection had seemed something in the distant future. Now, when he had decided to do the deed, Waldo had disappeared. An uneasiness had grown up between them since the death of Bianca, Primero said. Waldo had never been a confiding fellow, but he became withdrawn, almost accusatory. Did he blame his employer for acquiescing in the wild and independent life of the woman who was still his wife? Joseph would never have attempted an explanation, not of Waldo, not of anyone. He scarcely understood himself.

When he'd received the news that their child was dead, he had been unable to suppress the thought that Bianca was at fault. There was no evidence of this. She was scatterbrained, someone who seemed destined never fully to grow up, but that had been her attraction. Joseph had wanted to protect her, and when the child came he wanted to protect them both. But duty and honor have their claims and he was at sea when the news came. When he arrived home, during the moment before he took Bianca in his arms, when he saw the expression on her face, waiting to be accused, his heart broke. The anguish he felt could not be any deeper than hers. So they embraced and were more bound by the loss of their child than they were by their wedding vows. Or so it had seemed to him.

He surprised himself by the ease with which he disclosed the central fact of his life to Roger Knight. The massive professor acknowledged the confidence with a moment of silence before he spoke. "It wasn't very smart of Waldo to disappear," Roger said.

"I never understood why his going was described so dramatically, as if he had run away. He left my employ; that's all it was."

"Had you told him about transferring the collection immediately?"

"That isn't why he left."

"So what was the reason?"

"You would have to know Waldo Hermes to understand."

"He is here," Roger said.

Primero congratulated himself that he did not show the surprise and alarm he felt.

"Here?" When Roger nodded, there were sympathetic tremors throughout his body.

"He felt under suspicion. So he 'escaped.' The word is his. You wouldn't recognize him."

"How so?"

Primero managed to smile at the account of the missing beard, the shaved head, the great frog face relieved only by luxuriant eyebrows.

"The best disguise is the simplest."

"Like disappearing into a nudist colony," Philip said.

"I wouldn't pursue that thought, Philip," Roger chided. "I of course would simply blend into the ambience of flesh, but others might find it more difficult."

196

"You've talked with Waldo then."

"Oh yes. He was at dinner last night. If you had come, you could have been reunited with your former employee—before he goes off to the Trappists."

"The Trappists!"

"For a long visit, not to join."

This was upsetting news. Several times, Joseph Primero had confided to Waldo his sometime desire to leave everything and put the world behind him. He would go to a monastery. Once he had made a retreat with the Dominicans, and he had never forgotten it.

"Have you every been to a Trappist abbey?" Waldo had asked then.

Waldo had been a storehouse of information on the Cistercians, but then he was the repository of endless amounts of arcane knowledge, picked up God knows where over a lifetime of scholarship. At the table in The Morris Inn, Roger's remark about Waldo's plans struck Joseph Primero as a mockery of his own dreams and somehow threatening.

"Waldo and I must get together. Does he know I'm here?"

"Yes."

"How can I get in touch with him?"

Roger seemed to hesitate. "I can tell him you want to see him."

"If I am not in my room, have him leave a message."

He said good-bye to the Knights in the lobby. It was agreed that Philip had successfully completed the job he had been asked to do.

"Everything but catch the thief," Philip said.

"With everything recovered, that is less important than it was."

"It seems that your wife gave a key to the Lake of the Isles house to Dudley."

Primero did not comment. He regretted now inviting all this professional curiosity to scrutinize his affairs. Of course the police, and the Knights, would think it had been Waldo, and he realized that he had not done much to discourage this line of inquiry, but Waldo could not be in any real danger.

When they parted, he went upstairs to his room. He had found the lunch disquieting, threatening the euphoria he had felt since arriving on campus. What on earth was Waldo doing here? He had struck up an acquaintance with the assistant archivist Whelan. What else would have drawn him to Notre Dame? The collection was still in Minneapolis, under a twenty-four-hour security guard now. News of the theft had not been widespread, but wily thieves did not need headlines to find new places to strike.

His window gave him a view of one of the older residence halls. He looked it up on the campus map, Alumni Hall. Generations of students had lived in those rooms. Primero longed to have a closer connection with this university. That was the meaning of giving his collection to Notre Dame and speeding up the process was an indication of the urgency he felt to belong here, to belong somewhere. Where did he belong? The house on Lake of the Isles had been turned into a museum by Bianca's leaving. His penthouse at the condominium he seldom used. It would have been more practical to rent it, but being practical had long since ceased to be a motive.

"You sure?" Norma had asked, when he told her he wanted the security videos destroyed.

"What's the point of keeping them?"

"The police have asked about them."

"Is there anything on them that would help their investigation?"

"That's for them to say."

"Anything you couldn't tell them yourself?"

"It's mainly tape that looks like stills, then people entering."

"I had forgotten we had that system installed."

"You could keep the ones you're on."

"Ha."

"Your nickname was 'Smilin' Jack.' "

"Why?"

"Scarf, crushed cap, leather jacket."

"I don't have a leather jacket."

"I imagine that part; I imagined the scarf too."

Norma was a strange girl. "Your job must be very boring."

"Between murders." Her expression changed. "I'm sorry."

"Let me have the videos." Norma could tell the police about the penthouse, she could tell them about his comings and goings. Even so, he wanted the videos.

36

GREG WHELAN REVEALED TO
Roger Waldo's proximate reason for aban-
doning his job as curator of the Primero Collection, disguising himself with his razor, and lighting out for South Bend.

"He says Primero knows who stole those items."

"Dudley Fyte?"

"He says it's far more complicated than that."

So Roger stopped by Greg's apartment to see Waldo Hermes,
being admitted only after a long rigamarole at the door.

"Waldo, it's Roger Knight."

"I can see that. Are you alone?"

"Yes."

"How do I know?"

"You can take my word."

A full minute of silence went by before the door was opened, the
chain still in place. Finally, Roger was given entry to Greg's apartment.

"Who are you frightened of?"

"Is it true that Joseph Primero is in town?"

"I just had lunch with him."

"Does he know I'm here?"

"Yes, I told him."

"I don't want to see him."

"Waldo, tell me about it." He paused. "Tell me what you told
Greg."

"Primero led you to believe that I might be the thief, didn't he?"

"Waldo, Bianca gave Dudley Fyte a key to the house so that he could steal those things. The most likely thief is Dudley Fyte."

Waldo thought about it, working his wide mouth and rubbing his head. Now that his cover had been blown, so to speak, he had returned to the smelly, unlit pipe through which he preferred to filter the air of the world. It bubbled now as he thought.

"Even if it happened just that way, there is more . . ."

"I'm listening."

"Joseph Primero is right. I am responsible for the theft. I just thank God everything has been recovered."

"From Bianca's car, Waldo. In a briefcase belonging to Dudley Fyte. Why do you say you're responsible for the theft?"

"Because I told Bianca what items should be taken."

Waldo looked with wide, unblinking eyes at Roger, his expression one that all of us will wear at the Last Judgment.

"I played the role of Judas."

"Tell me everything."

Roger felt like a confessor listening to Waldo's story. It began with the early days of his employment by Joseph Primero.

"He had warned me that his wife would resent my presence, but I was simply to do my job and ignore her. She chose not to ignore me."

Waldo's eyes grew wider. Roger nodded, indicating he should continue.

"I didn't understand what was going on at first. She seemed interested in what I was doing, wanted to be told all about it. I was new to the collection, she had been living in the same house with it for years, and she was asking me the most basic questions."

But Bianca's aim soon became clear. She intended to seduce her husband's assistant.

"I was Samson to her Delilah, Roger."

"Well, you had the hair for it."

"I didn't wear a beard then, but my hair hung to my shoulders."

Bianca put Waldo at ease by seeking information from him in the library during the day.

"The first time she looked into my bedroom over the garage, I almost levitated. It was nearly midnight. She said she had a question."

The oldest question of all. They answered it there on Waldo's bachelor bed. Afterward, from the moment she slipped away and left him to his thoughts, Waldo was riven with remorse. First of all, he had sinned mortally. He had slept with a married woman. He had committed adultery. That it was his first experience with a woman made it seem worse.

"My first and last. I took a vow. I knelt beside my bed and for the rest of the night I prayed. I promised that if I were forgiven, if I could confess my sins, I would live as a celibate for the rest of my life."

"As a penance?"

"As a penance. I had betrayed God. I had betrayed myself. I had betrayed Joseph Primero, a good man with a bad wife." Waldo let out an enormous sigh. "And I would betray him again."

"How did Bianca react to your vow?"

"I told her only that we could never again do what we had done."

"And?"

"She laughed. She said she had been going to tell me that once was all I got, and I shouldn't make a pest of myself."

"That must have been a relief."

"It should have been. I confessed my sins and I have kept my vow. But the presence of Bianca in the house was almost more than I could endure. It soon became clear to me that she traveled in

202

order to find transient partners. That prompted me to make the biggest mistake of my life. No, the second biggest. I decided to tell Joseph what had happened between Bianca and me."

"Dear God."

"It seemed to be the only way I could convince him of Bianca's infidelity."

"What did he say?"

"It's what he didn't say. I expected to be fired on the spot. I would have accepted that because it would have meant he understood what kind of wife he had. But he only nodded. When he spoke it was softly. He told me to go back to work."

If he said nothing to Waldo, he must have spoken to Bianca. A frigid silence settled over the house. It ended only when Bianca decided to have her own apartment in Highland Village.

"He helped her get it. He had built the place. He is still part owner. That seemed to indicate that he was repudiating her. But it was she who was doing the repudiating. And he colluded with her. I tried to think of it as Christian, but it was craven. He was aiding and abetting her infidelity."

Primero seemed to Waldo to become ever more supine. His passivity merely increased Bianca's misbehavior, which now seemed to have the public humiliation of her husband as its goal. It was this that Waldo had hoped to bring to an end. He wanted Primero finally to see what Bianca was and to repudiate her once and for all.

"That is why I betrayed him again."

He managed to get in touch with Bianca, overcoming her reluctance to talk with him. Waldo had kept au courant on her activities, something easy enough to do she was so brazen about it. He knew about her prolonged liaison with Dudley Fyte.

"When I did talk with her, I told her I was leaving her husband's employ. This appealed to her curiosity. She wanted to know why."

Waldo's story of his disaffection with the job, his resentment at his treatment by Joseph Primero—all his complaints imaginary—seemed music to Bianca's ears.

"So why are you telling me this?"

"I have been thinking of a dramatic departure."

And so began the great betrayal that was motived by loyalty to Joseph Primero. Bianca had used Waldo; now Waldo would use Bianca. She saw immediately how the theft of the most precious items in Joseph's collection would devastate him.

"You'll pass them on to me?"

"That wouldn't be convincing. No, they have to be taken from the house and while I am not there."

"You expect me to go there? I wouldn't know what to take."

"Is there someone you could trust?"

She thought for a moment. "Perhaps. But how would he know what to take?"

"Do you have a pen?"

He dictated to her the items and their location. Then there was silence. He assumed she would enlist Dudley Fyte in the escapade. In subsequent days, he became aware of Bianca's Jaguar driving slowly past, usually with a passenger. And then the young man drove by alone. How could Waldo be out of the house if he did not know when the theft would take place?

He learned about it only after it had taken place. One morning he went into the library and saw the telltale gaps in the shelves. He went immediately to Joseph Primero. "And he got in touch with your brother."

"Well, your plan seemed to have had the desired effect. Not that the end justifies the means."

But the whole object was compromised by Primero's decision *not* to tell the police that he had been robbed. That seemed symbolic of his denial of Bianca's flamboyant infidelity.

"Roger, I thought the items would be recovered immediately from Bianca's apartment and that would be it as far as Joseph and Bianca were concerned. Maybe it wouldn't matter that the police weren't involved or that criminal charges were not brought. He would no longer be able to ignore what she was."

But the items had not been recovered in Bianca's apartment, but in her car in Dudley's briefcase, pointing the guilt to him. Waldo tried not to sound critical of the Knight brothers, but his disappointment was obvious. He had told them Bianca was responsible; they should have proceeded full steam ahead.

"But you dithered. Or Phil did."

"Did you expect him to break into her apartment?"

"Isn't that the sort of thing private detectives do. Anyway, I decided to add fuel to the fire."

"And sent those Newman letters to Notre Dame?"

"Now you can understand why I fled Minneapolis. I could no longer face the man I had betrayed twice. And, coward that I am, I feared for myself. He was bound to accuse me, and then I could only get it off my chest."

Instead, he had made a bare face and a bare head of it and headed for South Bend, the ultimate destination of the treasures whose custodian he had been.

Phil sat on the edge of his chair, his bottle of beer dangling between his knees, listening to Roger's report on Waldo's claim that it was the custodian who had initiated the theft from the Primero Collection.

"That's hard to believe, Roger."

"Not when you hear him tell it."

Phil sent a message to Swenson, asking him to call. There might be a big breakthrough in the Bianca Primero case.

"What the hell do you mean, 'breakthrough'?" Swenson asked when he called later that night.

"Maybe Dudley didn't kill her."

"Maybe? Look, we have built a strong case; the prosecutor is eager to try Dudley and is convinced he can get a conviction."

"He may be right."

"All right then?"

"But you want to be sure that he did what he would be convicted of."

"He won't confess, I'll tell you that. He insists he is innocent, but what's new?"

Phil patiently laid out for Swenson the elements of Waldo Hermes's account. The theft had looked like an inside job from the beginning, drawing suspicion to the curator.

"Knight, I couldn't care less about those books. My worry is that the coroner is going to do another flip and decide that Bianca Primero's death was suicide."

37 THE FOLLOWING DAY AT eleven-thirty, Roger drove his golf cart to Sacred Heart Basilica and slowly climbed the stairs to the main door. He levered it open and stepped inside. As the great door closed softly behind him, he looked over the massive font of holy water just inside the inner doors and then up the aisle toward the sanctuary. There was an altar facing the congregation, as was typical after Vatican II, but beyond it was the pre–Vatican II altar that Father Sorin had brought back from a eucharistic conference in Philadelphia. It had been love at first sight; Father Sorin knew immediately that such an altar belonged in the campus church at Notre Dame. So he bought it and had it shipped home and placed where it had stood ever sense, a baroque golden dream of an altar, with towering tabernacle and carved saints and angels occupying positions of honor on its lower and upper levels. The glittering altar, matching the gilt decorations of the church, did not completely arrest the eye, which went on to the statue of the Virgin set in its niche above the Bernini altar at the far end of the apse. It was a breathtaking sight, and Roger never saw it without a leap of the heart.

He took a seat. A lector was in the pulpit, and the readings of the day echoed in the acoustically unfriendly church. Fr. Peter Rocca, the rector of the Basilica, was the celebrant. He sat at the right of the altar, following the readings. Perhaps they were audible to him. When he took the pulpit to read the Gospel of the day and give his homily, every word was clear and audible. It was when the congregation stood for the reading of the Gospel that Roger saw Joseph Primero in a front pew.

When Mass was over, Roger waited for Primero, who made a lengthy thanksgiving. Afterward, he walked toward the front of the church, wanting to see the baroque altar in the Lady Chapel, all white and gold, looking edible. He would have to come back through the sanctuary, so Roger rose and moved toward the front of the church, seating himself conspicuously in the front row. Even at that, he had to stand in order for Joseph Primero to notice him.

The collector came toward Roger smiling. "Don't tell me I'll have the pleasure of taking you to lunch two days in a row."

"No. I will take you."

They went in Roger's cart to Cafe de Grasta, a restaurant on the first floor of Grace Hall, now full of administrative offices.

"More modest than The Morris Inn, but the food is good."

They carried their trays to a table looking out on the snowy campus. Primero was delighted to be shown another aspect of Notre Dame.

"It is the past of the place that interests me even more than its present," Roger said.

"Its history."

"Yes. Have you visited the grave of Orestes Brownson?"

"He is buried here?"

"In the lower church, in the main aisle."

The critic of Cardinal Newman's theory of the development of doctrine had been a favorite of Father Sorin—though not for that reason.

"I must look up what he had to say of the *Apologia*," Roger mused. "If he was alive when it appeared."

"He could hardly take exception to that."

208

"What a relief it must be to have your first edition safely back."

"Yes."

"Odd that it should have shown up where it did. In the trunk of your wife's car."

Primero did not answer. Three chattering secretaries at the next table provided background music.

"Have you been following the fate of young Dudley Fyte?" Roger asked.

A look of pain. "The worst thing about the loss of Bianca is that it does not stop. There is the constant reminder."

"Fyte still insists that he is innocent."

"Of what? Does he admit any guilt?"

"He is not being accused of adultery."

"That was the source of his troubles."

"And your wife's."

"It would be a terrible thing if he were found guilty of the wrong crime."

"If there is a crime."

"What do you mean?"

"Swenson, whom you've met, told Phil last night that he fears the coroner may still declare the death a suicide."

"That's nonsense!"

"It could save Dudley Fyte."

"They told me they were sure he was guilty." Primero was disturbed and excited.

"We are all guilty."

This unassailable theological truth received a contrapuntal laugh from one of the secretaries. La Grasta was not the best place for a conversation about crime and punishment. They finished their meal and rode back to The Morris Inn in silence, wending their way through students, many of them with heads down against the chill wind. Primero said something Roger did not hear but waved it off when he asked him to repeat it. When he got out of the cart at the door of The Morris Inn, Roger asked Primero what he had said.

"I said this is as cold as Minnesota."

"Sure as God made little green apples. Do you know the song?"

Primero shook his head. "Would you ask your brother to come see me?"

"Of course."

Three hours later, when Roger was at his computer in communication with a semioticist in Helsinki, Phil called.

"Roger, an astounding thing. Joseph Primero has confessed."

"To what?"

"He says that he killed his wife. He wants me to go back to Minneapolis with him so he can turn himself in."

38

JOSEPH PRIMERO MADE AN ideal murderer. He publicly apologized to Dudley Fyte for having put him through this ordeal. He expressed his regret for allowing the police even to suspect that his longtime and valued assistant Waldo Hermes could possibly have been involved in the theft of items from the collection in his care. As for the death of his wife, he threw himself on the mercy of God. From the state, he expected nothing but justice.

Any disruption this caused the detective bureau and the prosecutor was tolerable because now all the pieces of the puzzle fit so neatly together. And there was a confession. Primero would of course plead innocent, and his confession would not be allowable in court, but it was public and highly publicized knowledge, and one could have gone to the ends of the earth—or at least of Ramsey County—and not impaneled a jury that did not know it. Primero's lawyer must of course go through the motions of defending him, using every legal device and angle to do so. Georges Simenon once said that if he were innocent, he would prefer to be tried in England; but if he were guilty, he would prefer to be tried in the United States. But Primero seemed almost to regret the precautions and checks built into the legal system. Guilty as he said he was, it would be necessary to prove this in a court of law.

"Even Jack Cousey should be able to do that," Swenson said. "I was never really confident that he could nail Fyte."

This was the first expression of such doubt, but no matter. Swenson's department and the prosecutor's office were suffused with the sense that there was but one possible outcome of the Primero trial. They relished the publicity given the fall of the wealthy developer of resorts and collector of rare books. What did wealth and erudition mean when his wife had deserted him for dissipation and a younger man? Dudley Fyte, erstwhile gigolo, was transformed into a celebrity by the turn of events. His folly, or more likely venality, in becoming linked to such a woman as Bianca Primero had provided inspiration for newspaper piece after newspaper piece. A cable station, sensing a trend in spring/autumn affairs, had interviewed him as he awaited trial. The antinomian sympathy of the interviewer elicited from Dudley one banality after another. He was led into a discussion of his childhood and threw caution to the winds, revealing his Nebraska roots. A former classmate recognized him, and the change of name to Dudley Fyte was mocked and joked about. One might have been given such a name and that was fate, but to choose it? That quickly, he was once more a figure of fun. But the confession of Joseph Primero again transformed Dudley's status.

"As a lawyer, I wonder how many guilty men go free and how many innocent ones are punished," he said unctuously to the reporters who met him when he stepped into freedom.

But for the nonce, Dudley was pushed offstage and Joseph Primero was in the spotlight. His motive could not have been more obvious. A cuckold, embarrassed privately and publicly by his wife's behavior, he had reached a point where he could honorably take no more. He strangled his wife and then, the memory of love returning, arranged her on her bed and bade her a last adieu.

The theft of some of his rare books? A ruse perpetrated by himself out of confused and equivocal motivation. Would the loss of those valuable items spark some sympathy in Bianca's breast? There were of course other interpretations of the relation between the theft and the murder. The theft had been a smokescreen. Primero had meant to turn attention away from himself and to set off a search for the thief who had turned murderer.

"I never dreamed that suspicion would fall on Dudley Fyte."

Incredulity greeted this remark. Primero began to be seen as a calculating and cagey character. He had hoped Waldo Hermes would be suspected. He had known that sooner or later it would occur to someone that Bianca's key to the house could have been provided to Dudley Fyte. His eventual confession ceased to seem altruistic. He had been driven to speak by his conscience.

"Of course our investigation was ongoing, to clear up loose ends," Swenson told the press. "I suppose that unnerved him."

"When did you start suspecting him?"

"In this kind of investigation, everyone is a suspect."

Phil was at Primero's side while he was questioned; his lawyer, Daniels, on the other side. Primero spoke slowly and with deliberation as if for years he had been rehearsing for this moment. How often must he not have thought of doing violence to the woman who had made such a fool of him? The fact that he had a penthouse apartment in the condominium where Bianca lived had masochistic elements to it, as if he wanted to be a witness to his own humiliation. He came and went more often than would have been suspected. Norma could testify to that.

"She called me 'Smilin' Jack.' I suppose I did half disguise myself, as if everyone would know why I was there."

"But she didn't know Bianca was your wife."

"Didn't she? I assumed she did. I suppose I assumed everyone knew of my disgrace."

The penthouse was held in the name of the construction company Primero owned: Edification Inc. It permitted him to come and go at will.

"Only if I drove through the gate would Norma know I was there. Of course one could also approach the building by foot and admit oneself by key."

This had been the strong part of the case against Dudley Fyte. The discovery of keys to the building and to Bianca's apartment found in his car, the fact that he had signed in and out, placing himself in the building when Bianca was murdered, had not moved him to confess.

"First, it's books, now it's keys. Bianca never gave me keys to that place."

Nor did he admit to having signed in and out of the building. But Primero smoothed the way by admitting the use of a key. And he enlarged his apology to Dudley Fyte. He had written his name in the book, expertly imitating the signatures it already contained.

"And I put those keys in his car. And filled his briefcase with the missing items."

"Why did you have the tapes destroyed?"

Primero looked rueful. "They were mine. I could do with them what I wished. No one had subpoenaed them."

That didn't answer the question that had been asked, but they let it go.

Philip, reporting on these events to Roger in South Bend, felt sorry for Primero and knew that he himself had gone more than an extra mile for the client who had hired him to investigate a theft from his collection.

Roger had a request. "Phil, get hold of the coroner's report on Bianca Primero."

"What for?"

"Please."

Phil sighed. "I'll see what I can do."

Several hours later he faxed the report to Roger.

39

FATHER CARMODY WAS SHOCKED by the turn of events in the Primero matter. It had been bad enough that the wife of a university benefactor had been murdered and her illicit lover accused of the crime, but now to have Joseph Primero himself confess to the murder of his wife!

"Uxoricide!" the old priest barked, as if the arcane word added to Primero's perfidy. "It's absolutely certain that he confessed?"

Roger assured him that it was.

"We had an opportunity to talk while he was here," Father Carmody said. "We talked about everything, his life, his marriage. He put an interesting point to me. When does a man's toleration of his wife's misbehavior pass the point of charity and become stupidity?"

"Most men would not have the problem."

Carmody nodded. "He considered himself weak. Here he was, a very successful man, first in the navy, then as a developer, finally capping it off with a keen amateur's knowledge of the rare book market. And he was putty in his wife's hands. Was it long-suffering or simply moral weakness? Turning the other cheek, forgiving seventy times seven, or colluding with her weakness? He was never able to decide."

Roger looked at the old priest. "Joseph and I talked while he was here but not about such things."

"A priest is made privy to many things, Roger." There was puzzlement in Carmody's voice. Roger sensed that they might have entered an area where he might not intrude.

"And can absolve."

Carmody shook his head. "It wasn't a confession in that sense."

The faxed autopsy came in while Father Carmody was visiting, and they looked it over together. The cause of death was strangulation. Phil had got hold of the preliminary coroner's report as well, and Roger puzzled over these documents after the priest had gone back to his room in Corby Hall. After a time, Roger lay both reports by his computer and stared at the blank monitor. The two reports agreed that death could have been caused by strangulation, but one was more convincing than the other. They both showed the presence in the stomach and bloodstream of high amounts of both alcohol and sedatives.

After a time, Roger lifted the phone and called Phil. "I want to come up there, Phil. How can I do it?"

This was a problem. Roger did not drive, and even if he had it would have been unwise for him to set off for the Twin Cities in their van, the roads and weather being as chancy as they were. As for flying, that was always a problem—getting Roger to the airport, getting him two seats instead of one.

"I'll call you back."

When Phil did call back, he had the solution. Joseph Primero was touched at Roger's desire to be with him during his ordeal. He would send his own plane for Roger and arranged for an escort service to pick him up and take him to the Michiana Regional Transportation Center.

Mere hours later, Roger was in Minneapolis with his brother.

Joseph Primero was a man at peace. He took Roger's hand, and his beatific expression said how grateful he was to see him. They were alone in the conference room in the courthouse jail.

"Our talks at Notre Dame were a great help, Roger."

"Your confession surprised me."

"I can't tell you what a great relief it has been to stop pretending."

"Tell me about it, Joseph."

Primero cocked his head. "Tell you about it? I would rather forget it."

"There is small chance of that now."

"You're right, you're right. So where should I begin?"

"When you arrived at Bianca's apartment on the day she died."

"That is quickly told. I came into . . ."

"You let yourself in."

Primero hesitated, then nodded, "Yes."

"Where did you find her?"

"Find her?"

"Was she in the bathroom, in the bedroom, on the floor of the living room?"

Primero sat back, looking warily at Roger. "What are you getting at?"

"The coroner's preliminary report and the autopsy indicate a good deal of sedatives in your wife's system. And alcohol in her blood."

"I'm not surprised."

"What did you think when you found her?"

"Why do you insist on that turn of phrase?"

"She did die by strangulation, Joseph. That is clear from both reports: the coroner's initial examination and the autopsy."

218

"And I did it."

"Killed her? I don't think you realized at the time that that is what you were doing."

After a moment, Primero's mouth formed a joyless smile. "You are an interesting fellow, Roger."

"Not nearly so interesting as yourself. Will you tell me about it now?"

"It doesn't make the slightest difference anymore."

"Legally? Perhaps not."

"Roger, what set your mind going on this?"

"A talk I had with Father Carmody. He mentioned the long conversations the two of you had during your visit to Notre Dame."

"But I told him nothing."

"That is what set my mind going. If you felt guilty of murder, you would have confessed to a priest before you confessed to the police."

"Tell me what you think happened."

"I think you found your wife unconscious, signs that she had been drinking, and then a bottle of sleeping tablets beside her. You thought she had committed suicide." When Primero said nothing, Roger went on. "That would have been the ultimate betrayal, not of you, but of God. You wanted to spare her that dreadful judgment. So you arranged a murder scene. And you strangled her. Her dead body, as you thought."

After a long minute of silence, Primero said, "It was the constant waffling on how she had died. And when you told me that the coroner was again leaning toward suicide, well, that settled it."

"But you thought it was suicide at the time?"

There was a long silence. On Primero's face a whole catechism of the truths by which he lived was fleetingly present and there was an infinite sadness in his eyes. But then he almost brightened.

219

"Thank God I was wrong."

Roger let it go. Joseph Primero had the right to any small consolation he could derive from the way his wife had died. How could she be a suicide if he had killed her?

EPILOGUE

MRS. TORRE WAS GLAD THAT
the manager of The Morris Inn seemed not to
notice that the name of the groom had been changed. Dolores
thought that balanced the fact that she and Larry were now claiming the reservation at Sacred Heart Basilica as originally made. In
any case, with the reception already scheduled, Mrs. Torre had lots
of time for the Warren Golf Course.

When the Knight brothers received their invitation to the wedding, it created a difficulty.

"It would be disloyal to Nancy," Phil said.

"You just don't like to go to weddings."

"June 17 was the day Larry Morton was going to marry Nancy.
Now he's going to marry Dolores on that day. And in Sacred Heart."

Roger was amused by Phil's suddenly sensitive conscience. "I'll
talk to Nancy."

"I'm going myself; I wouldn't miss it." Nancy was more animated
than Roger had ever seen her.

"You're not at all bothered by the way things have turned out?"

"Good heavens, no. Obviously he never really loved me."

"That's going pretty far."

"Maybe what I felt for him was less than love too."

Onto the unfathomable ocean of male/female relations Roger was unwilling to embark. But the truth was that Nancy did seem relieved that it was Dolores Larry would marry on June 17 and not herself. "Frailty thy name is woman?" Then what of Larry?

If Nancy was forgiving, her mother was incensed. "He sat in this house, he ate at this table, he was smooth as butter, and all the time . . ."

"All the time he wanted margarine," grumped Professor Beatty. But he was quite content with the way things had turned out.

"Imagine turning down scholarships that will carry her through to her doctorate! I felt like disowning her when she told me she wanted to marry that—that lawyer."

"Now she'll become a professor like her father."

Beatty tried not to show the pleasure the thought gave him. "It's no longer a full-time job, as I can admit to you. She can marry as well. Later."

There was no question of the Beattys attending the wedding, of course, so Nancy went with the Knight brothers.

The day of the wedding the weather was glorious. Sun streamed through the campus trees, glinted off the golden dome, made the bride's dress seem even whiter than it was. After the nuptial Mass, the couple came squinting into the sunlight and stood on the steps of the Basilica to receive one more round of applause from their friends and guests.

"She looks beautiful," Nancy said.

"At least he's marrying someone his own age."

She punched Phil in the ribs. "Watch out or I'll marry you."

Joshing about a discrepancy of ages sent Roger's mind back to the ill-fated Dudley Fyte and Bianca Primero. Dudley had disappeared from the Minneapolis scene; his vindication of all charges had not smoothed his way back into the good graces of Kunert and Skye. There was the public scandal of his affair with Bianca. And there was his name. Dudley Fyte had been a fanciful name to adopt, but the media had made his real name known—Dungman, Francis Dungman. The country had moved far from its rural roots but not far enough to erase the associations of that name.

Phil took Nancy on to the reception, but Roger begged off. He wanted to stop by Holy Cross House and talk with Father Carmody. As he directed his golf cart along the road to Moreau Seminary and continued on to the retirement home, Roger thought of the strange events that seemed to have reached their end in the wedding he had just attended.

"Waldo thinks he might stay at New Melleray," Greg Whelan had confided to Roger.

"And become a monk?"

"The library there sounds amazing. They need someone to look after it, and the librarian has to be a monk. Of course he would only be on probation at first."

"As librarian?"

"That's what I said."

If Greg had any deficiency, it was a less than lively sense of humor. Or was he relieved at the permanent removal of a threat to his presiding over the Primero Collection? In the new building that was planned, he would have a whole floor to himself. Notre Dame turned out to be the major beneficiary of Joseph Primero's conviction for the murder of his wife. He had signed over 90 percent of his wealth to the university.

Father Carmody was sitting in a lawn chair, scowling across the lake at the university. "It's a regular skyline now," he groused. "There won't be a foot of free land if they keep this up."

Roger sat on the bench he had dragged up beside Carmody's chair. There was a sweet scent in the air; there was the constant twitter of birds. On the lake below them, the sail of a small boat caught the breeze and moved hypnotically from east to west.

"Joseph Primero was sentenced yesterday," Roger said.

"Do they have the death penalty in Minnesota?"

"Oh, there was never any danger of that. He may be a free man before you know it."

Carmody looked at Roger. "He asked me once if there were provisions for people like himself retiring at Notre Dame."

"Maybe he'll come here when he gets out."

Carmody lost interest in the subject. If that happened, he would have already claimed his place in the community cemetery. But he perked up when Roger told him the details of the death of Bianca Primero. It posed the kind of problem in moral theology Father Carmody liked.

"He thought she was already dead?"

"He thought she had committed suicide. It was to cover that up that he strangled her."

"Thinking he was strangling a dead woman?"

"To save her reputation." Carmody looked sharply at Roger. Bianca Primero's reputation had hardly been all it should be.

"How did he react when he learned what had actually happened?"

"I think he prefers his own version."

Again the old priest gave Roger a sharp look. "He would rather be a murderer than have his wife be a suicide."

"But he isn't a murderer, not morally. Not if he did what he did simply to prevent a judgment of suicide."

"That doesn't help, legally."

"But surely the sentence was less severe because of the circumstances."

"He didn't tell his lawyer what he thought he was doing."

Father Carmody sighed. "So he will go on suffering because of that woman."

"Any suffering he feels is relieved by knowing that she did not kill herself. He did."

"But if she intended to kill herself . . ."

"That's unlikely, Father." The ironies continue. Swenson had gathered evidence against Dudley Fyte that suggests Fyte had dosed Bianca's drink with what, in conjunction with the alcohol, should have been enough sedatives to kill her.

"You mean the real murderer gets off free."

"He tried but failed to murder her."

"But attempted homicide is a crime."

The conversation went on, as such conversations will. Later, whenever Roger Knight thought of the Primeros, he was put in mind of the moral maxims Father Carmody kept repeating there on the lawn overlooking the lake. A person can be guilty of something he did not do. And innocent of what he did.